Dear Readers,

We're so excited to release our new book series, Sprouse Bros. 47 R.O.N.I.N.! When we decided to develop a book series, we wanted to create stories kids our age would love. So we jam-packed our series with all of the cool things we love to read about—top secret plots, ninja fighters, ancient samurai weapons, and ultimate villains. We even have a lot in common with the main characters, Tom and Mitch, from our favorite desserts to our favorite bands. Because we love comics so much, we've included original comic book–style art—illustrated by an awesome comic book artist—in each book. We think it rocks, and we hope you do too!

Thanks for reading our series, and stay tuned for future episodes of Sprouse Bros. 47 R.O.N.I.N.!

Dylan Sprouse and Cole Sprouse

We would like to thank our dad and our manager, Josh, for their constant support. Thanks also to everyone at Dualstar and Simon & Schuster for all of their hard work. Last, but not least, thanks to all of our friends and fans—this is for you guys!

—Dylan Sprouse and Cole Sprouse

SIMON SPOTLIGHT

An imprint of Simon & Schuster Children's Publishing Division • 1230 Avenue of the Americas, New York, New York 10020

Sprouse Bros.™ and related *Sprouse Bros.* trademarks are trademarks of DC Sprouse Inc., and licensed exclusively by Dualstar Entertainment Group, LLC. © 2007. DC Sprouse, Inc. All rights reserved. • All rights reserved, including the right of reproduction in whole or in part in any form.

SIMON SPOTLIGHT and colophon are registered trademarks of Simon & Schuster, Inc.

Manufactured in the United States of America • First Edition   10 9 8 7 6 5 4 3 2 1

ISBN-13: 978-1-4169-3800-2 • ISBN-10: 1-4169-3800-1

Library of Congress Catalog Card Number 2007921587

47 r·o·n·i·n·

EPISODE 2 THE SHOWDOWN

by Marc Cerasini
with Dylan Sprouse and Cole Sprouse

based on the series concept created by Marc Cerasini
with Dylan Sprouse and Cole Sprouse

illustrated by Lawrence Christmas

Simon Spotlight
New York London Toronto Sydney

Unless you enter the tiger's den,
you cannot take the cubs.
—Japanese proverb

PROLOGUE

Tom Hearn hunkered down behind a decaying log. His clothes were stained with sweat and his breathing came in gulps. Around him a weak breeze rustled the trees. As the sun began to rise, songbirds fluttered among the branches. Dull yellow columns of light broke through the leafy canopy, but the forest floor was still immersed in quiet darkness.

The sudden pounding of running feet made Tom tense—until he saw that it was his brother. Diving out of the brush, Mitch landed beside Tom on the stony ground.

For this mission, Mitch was dressed exactly like his brother. His loose camouflaged overalls covered his form from neck to boot tops. His hair was tucked under a black knit cap, and olive-colored paint was smeared over his cheeks and broad forehead. It was one of the few times in their lives that the brothers didn't object to dressing exactly the same.

Tom and Mitch were identical twins. When they were too little to object, their late mother had often put them in cutesy coordinated outfits. At fifteen they wouldn't have been caught dead sharing the same clothes, even though they obviously shared the same features: fair complexions with a smattering of freckles across the nose, blue eyes, and light blond hair worn in shaggy mops.

Before their training, Tom had been more built up than his brother. Unlike Tom, however, Mitch had never been that into sports and martial arts. Computers, gadgets, and all manner of cybertech gear had always been his thing. But even wiry Mitch had grown muscles after weeks in the field.

"I could use a lemonade about now," Mitch huffed. "From the deli on Forty-eighth Street. Lots of ice, too."

Tom frowned at the memory. That whole scene seemed so far away. Since he and his brother had discovered they were members of the Rogue Operative Network Inter-National (or R.O.N.I.N.), their world had turned upside down.

Four weeks ago he and Mitch had been living normal lives in New York City, going to movies, riding the subway, hanging at the dojo, eating dinner with their computer salesman dad, cutting classes at school to get in some extra skateboarding time—

Okay, Tom admitted to himself, so the cutting classes part was just me.

All that didn't matter anyway. It was behind them now. After weeks of brutal training, the brothers had been assigned a vital task: Navigate this section of Japanese wilderness in a race to stop a ticking time bomb, located inside a pagoda not far away.

The mission was a test—not to mention hazardous to their health—and Tom was happy he didn't have to face it alone. Thank goodness his brother and their new friend Laura Ting were by his side—

Wait, thought Tom, remembering Laura. He glanced around. "Where is she?" he whispered to his brother.

Mitch frowned. "I thought she was with you."

The quiet was broken by a trio of black helicopters. They buzzed back and forth in a methodical search pattern. Tom knew who they were searching for. He grabbed Mitch's arm.

"We have to go back for Laura," he rasped.

A soft voice called out suddenly, "I'm right here."

Laura Ting waved at them from a nearby bush. Like the brothers, she wore body armor, a battle dress uniform, and her face was camouflaged, her eyes gleaming behind the olive paint.

"Come on," Tom whispered. "It's clear."

Laura hurried to join them, darting across the ground in a running crouch.

"The bad guys are behind us and moving fast," she warned.

"Yeah, I counted six of them, armed with crossbows," whispered Mitch.

Bad news, Tom thought. Their only equipment was on their belts. Each of them had a length of coiled rope and a short utility knife.

"We have to keep moving," he said aloud. "The bomb's going off if we don't get to it. The pagoda where it's located should be ahead of us, across that empty space and through the trees."

Mitch peered at the barren stretch of ground. "Well, we can't go through that clearing. The helicopters will spot us. We'll have to circle around."

"No time," Tom replied. "I know it's risky, but we can cross the open ground quickly. Once we make it to the trees, we'll be under cover again. The choppers will never find us."

"Are you mental?" said Mitch. "What you're proposing isn't just *risky*, it's a death trap."

"Mitch is right," Laura agreed. "The helicopters will see us before we come close to making cover."

"Fine." Tom frowned at his brainy brother. He didn't like being second-guessed. "What do you suggest?"

"I'm not sure," Mitch replied, chewing his lip in thought. "I need more time to think about it."

Tom checked his wristwatch and exhaled in frustration. "Look. Don't you remember what Mr. Chance taught us?"

"I know, I know." Mitch nodded. "In a tight spot, it's better to act boldly than not at all."

Since the boys were young, Mr. Chance had been employed by their father as a chauffeur, butler, and cook. All along, however, that had simply been the man's cover.

Mr. Chance was a member of R.O.N.I.N. and a right arm to their dad, a clan leader in the secret organization. Since their father's mysterious disappearance, Mr. Chance had become the boys' guardian and sensei. He was the reason they were on this mission in the first place.

Tom glanced upward. The buzz of the helicopters seemed to be drifting away. They were searching another part of the forest!

"Do you hear that?" Tom asked. "This is our chance."

"Okay," Mitch said, finally agreeing. "Let's do it."

But Laura was still not convinced. "I don't know, guys," she groaned. "I'm still not sure about this."

"Well, I am," said Tom. "And you know what? It takes only *one* of us to stop the bomb."

Laura frowned. "What does that mean? Two of us are expendable?"

"If we all scatter as we cross the clearing, one of us will have a better chance of getting through," Tom pointed out.

"But if we don't stick together, then—"

Laura was interrupted by a sound in the woods behind them.

"No more talk. Get ready to move," Tom commanded. "Mitch, break right. Laura, go left. I'm the fastest, so I'll take the middle."

Mitch usually argued about who ran faster, but not today.

"Don't stop or slow down, no matter what happens," Tom said. But as soon as they broke cover, a volley of crossbow bolts shot out of the trees. Tom felt a breeze as a shaft whistled past his ear. Then he heard Laura exclaim, "Ahh!"

Breaking his own rule, Tom glanced over his shoulder. An arrow had struck Laura! He watched as three more hit her, and she fell to the ground.

Over Tom's head, the helicopters shifted direction. Two veered right to hunt down his brother. The other came for him. Tom raced for the tree line.

The forest exploded with noise. The hunters were moving too, choosing speed over stealth. Meanwhile Tom reached the trees, sidestepping another arrow that narrowly missed his shoulder.

Tom moved fast, his boots hitting rocks and avoiding soil and clumps of grass. He didn't want to leave a trail for his pursuers to follow. Overhead, the helicopters were back, circling like impatient vultures.

Tom slipped between two gnarled trunks just as four men in black, form-fitting battle suits emerged from the brush. Tom tensed, waiting for arrows to strike.

Instead he heard a *SNAP!* then gasps. Tom turned to find his pursuers caught by a rope Mitch had strung between the trees.

"Run!" cried Mitch, clutching one end of the rope. Then a volley of arrows struck, throwing him backward.

Tom turned his back on his fallen brother and melted into the forest. The sound of beating blades faded as helicopters drifted farther away.

Ducking behind a twisted tree, Tom watched two men search the ground, trying to pick up his trail. When one approached his hiding place, Tom lashed out.

Slapping the crossbow aside, Tom used the palms of his hands to rain blows on the hunter's chin. The man groaned as he fell.

The noise attracted the attention of his partner, but before the other could react, Tom grabbed the fallen crossbow and pulled the trigger. The bolt struck its target. Tom was gone before the man hit the ground.

Between the trees he finally saw the Japanese pagoda, silhouetted by a rugged mountain. Tom hoped there was still enough time to stop the bomb. In his haste, he burst from cover before checking the sky. As he ran toward the pagoda, a helicopter roared into attack. Tom glanced up to see a bomb drop from the belly of the aircraft.

Instincts honed by weeks of training took over. Tom reversed direction and ran back down the hill, away from the plummeting bomb. He kept going until he heard the explosion, felt the first blast of heat and pressure against his back. Then he jumped, upward and forward, using the shock wave to gain distance. Like a leaf in a storm, he tumbled end over end.

Tom lifted his arms above his head, tucked his body into a crouch, and landed on his hands, arms bent to absorb the impact. He rolled onto his right shoulder and down the hill, grateful for the soft covering of grass.

An orange fireball filled the sky, but the main force of the explosion passed harmlessly over Tom's head.

Slightly bruised, Tom somersaulted to his feet. As the smoke cleared, he ran up the hill. Through a haze of shock and exhaustion, he saw the pagoda's front door, open wide. He took the stairs two at a time.

The bomb was planted in the center of the room—not much more than a clock with a large face, mounted on a steel drum containing explosives. Tom slammed the red plunger down with the palm of his hand and the clock immediately stopped.

From somewhere inside the pagoda, alarm bells rang, shattering the dawn and signaling the end of the exercise. Tom collapsed onto the polished floor.

The alarm bells battered his ears for another minute, then fell silent. Through tired eyes, Tom watched Mitch and Laura enter the pagoda, both splattered and dripping with red dye.

"Gross. I got paint in my hair again," Laura complained, fingering her crimsoned locks.

"Forget about the paint," said Tom. "I want to know who *won*."

"Nobody *won* because this was not a *game*," a stern voice proclaimed.

A previously invisible door in the wall opened and Mr. Chance emerged. His slight frame was encased in the same battle suit worn by the men who'd chased them. They also exited the door behind Mr. Chance. They were members of the Japanese army's elite Special Assault Team. One man rubbed a bruised jaw. Another was splattered with red dye.

In his night-black battle suit, Mr. Chance reminded Mitch of a comic-book villain. But in Mitch's eyes, there was nothing villainous about this man, who'd been part of Mitch and Tom's family since they were seven years old. It was Mr. Chance who'd revealed that their father, Jack Hearn, was a clan leader in the secret organization called R.O.N.I.N., and that Tom and Mitch had been destined from birth to become members too. When evil forces had threatened the boys' lives, it was Mr. Chance who had helped them face that danger and triumph.

In the past few weeks, Mr. Chance had also become their combat trainer. In that role, the Japanese man eyed the trio unsympathetically.

Mitch wiped paint from his chin. "So did we stop the clock or didn't we?"

"Your mission was a success," Mr. Chance announced, and Tom thought he could detect a hint of pride behind the man's gaze.

Tom and Mitch slapped hands. Laura sighed. "At least I didn't get painted for nothing," she said.

Mr. Chance focused his stare on the girl. "The next time you decide to sacrifice yourself, Ms. Ting, lead the enemy *away* from your teammates. That way your loss will not be completely pointless."

Laura frowned. "That makes me feel better."

"It wasn't her idea to run across the clearing," Tom protested. "I made the call."

"And you can't say it didn't work out in the

end," said Mitch, joining the argument.

"Perhaps you will both feel differently when you really do order someone to their death," Mr. Chance replied.

Mitch wasn't bothered by Mr. Chance's words. He whooped as he faced his brother. "Man, my rope worked perfectly," he said proudly.

"Yeah," muttered Tom. "And I messed up, big-time. The helicopter almost nailed me."

Mr. Chance nodded. "Stop. Look. Listen. It is second nature when you cross the street back home. Why can't you master that skill in combat?"

"I knew I had to move fast," Tom said lamely.

Mr. Chance shook his head. "Your haste nearly finished you. Had that been real napalm and not a substitute, you would be dead."

Mitch jumped in to defend his brother. "Nobody's perfect," he cried.

"Perfection would certainly not describe *your* performance," Mr. Chance pointed out. "If you'd run after you sprang your trap, you might have escaped. Instead you stayed around to see the results of your cleverness, and the soldiers took you out."

Mitch's grin evaporated. He slumped to the floor beside his brother. "We'll never finish our training," he moaned.

Mr. Chance smiled. "You are wrong, young sir. This was your *final* exercise. You are ready for your first real mission. We cannot wait any longer."

The brothers exchanged excited glances. Both secretly hoped their first mission would be to find their missing father.

Laura had her own reason to be happy. "Great!" she said with a grin. "I finally get to wear one of those supercool battle suits."

CHAPTER 1

THE EMPIRE HOTEL, TOKYO, JAPAN

"I look like a total dork in this stupid outfit!" Laura Ting cried. She shook her head at her reflection in the full-length mirror. "This is just so . . . *wrong*."

Accustomed to wearing cargos, hoodies, and cross-trainers on the streets of New York, Laura absolutely hated the new clothes she'd just been given.

The Matsu School uniforms had arrived that afternoon. Laura, Tom, and Mitch had found the outfits waiting for them in their room when they'd returned to the hotel, hungry and tired after their day of sightseeing. Mr. Chance had ordered them to try the clothing on for size. Dinner, he'd informed them, would come later.

Dressed in the shapeless white top with a wide blue collar, Laura felt like a comic-book character. The low-heeled black shoes and matching kneesocks looked seriously lame.

"And what's with this chipmunk?" she asked, looking at the gold-embossed crest on the jacket.

"That's not a chipmunk," replied Mitch, fingering the same emblem on his own school uniform. "It's Matsuki, the school mascot. He's a mythical creature, a kind of combination cat and dog. Didn't you read the manga Mr. Chance gave you?"

"I don't read comic books. And you didn't read it either," Laura said defensively. "It's written in Japanese."

"Okay," admitted Mitch, "but I did look at the awesome artwork."

"Well, I looked at the cover, and it seemed pretty silly—almost as silly as this Matsuki crest."

Laura examined her reflection again, then made a face. "Needless to say, this is *not* what I expected to wear on my very first mission."

With all her complaining, Laura hadn't noticed Tom staring at her. He'd seen her in battle fatigues for so many weeks he'd almost forgotten that she was a girl.

"Actually, Laura, I . . . I think you look kind of . . . cute," he stammered.

She frowned. "I look like a bank teller."

"Okay." Tom shrugged. "Then I'd like to make a withdrawal. Large bills, please."

Mitch whacked Tom upside the head. "You're not helping."

"Hey!" Tom protested. "Watch the hair." He'd taken pains that morning to smooth down an unruly cowlick. He didn't want it popping up again, or he'd have to spend another hour fixing his hair.

Mitch ignored Tom and turned back to Laura. "Don't feel bad," he tried to reassure her. "It's actually an honor to wear the uniform of the Matsu School. We're about to begin classes at the world's most exclusive school for computer geniuses in Japan—maybe the world."

Mitch picked up the Matsu School orientation "guide," which looked more like a two-hundred-plus-page training manual.

"It says here that the Matsu School occupies the top twenty floors of the fifty-story Matsu Cybernetics Tower in downtown Tokyo." He opened the book and read the description: "A glass-and-steel building crowned by an illuminated glass spire."

Laura glanced out the hotel window. High above the city streets, the skyscrapers of Tokyo gleamed. In the distance, she located the Matsu Tower, silhouetted by the setting sun.

"The school is a division of Matsu Cybernetics, which is the most cutting-edge high-tech computer company in Tokyo," Mitch continued. "Best of all, we actually get to attend classes there—for free! How cool is that?"

"The catch is that I have to go out in public in these hideous clothes," complained Laura. "At least you guys get to wear black suits that make you look handsome. Distinguished. Mature."

Tom grinned and struck a cover-model pose. "You're right. I do look handsome and distinguished. Maybe I'll bag the mission and become a model."

Mitch whacked him again. Tom whirled and tackled his brother. While they wrestled on the floor, Laura folded her arms. "Okay," she said, "maybe I was wrong about that *mature* part."

Mitch and Tom ended their tussle and readjusted their clothing.

"Can you believe this?" Mitch whined. "We're fifteen, and here we are wearing identical outfits again, like when we were in kindergarten."

Tom chuckled, but for all his kidding around, he wondered whether he'd be able to pull off appearing as though he belonged at the prestigious school. Sure, he looked the part, but making it at Matsu was going to take more than just fitting into the uniform.

"Seriously, you guys," he said, "I hope I can make this happen. You two are the cyber-geniuses. I'm a champ at computer games, but I couldn't tell you the first thing about how they work."

"Then you have two days to improve your skills, young sir," said a quiet voice from the doorway.

Mr. Chance entered, tray in hand. The aroma of freshly brewed tea filled the suite.

"Two days isn't much," Tom pointed out.

Mr. Chance began to fill three delicate porcelain cups. "I'm sure Mitch and Laura will be happy to help you get up to speed."

Just then the phone rang.

"Allow me," remarked Mr. Chance. Then he hurried through the doorway into his adjoining room to receive the call. "Yes? Hello, sir. Yes . . . where are you?"

As Mr. Chance listened to the person on the other end, the boys and Laura resumed their conversation.

"Sure, I can teach you some advanced programs," said Laura.

Mitch nodded and lightly punched his brother's shoulder. "We'll turn you into a computer nerd in no time."

"Sounds like fun," Tom said miserably.

"Oh, c'mon, it won't be that bad," Mitch assured his brother. "You might even enjoy it!"

"I doubt it," Tom replied, unconvinced. "Look, I'm just not into this stuff like you are. Besides, no one likes looking like the stupid kid in class. What if they kick me out? Then I won't be able to help with the mission."

"You're not stupid," Laura said, stepping in. "Let's just get to work; I'm sure if you just focus you'll be surprised how quickly you catch on."

"Well, at least I have you guys, a total nerd and a complete genius, to help me!" Tom said, sounding reassured.

"Hey," Mitch protested. "Why am *I* a nerd when *she* gets to be a genius?"

This time it was Tom who did the whacking. Mitch winced from the playful blow. "Dude," Tom replied, "don't you know *anything* about women?"

Just then they heard Mr. Chance speak again, for the first time in minutes. "No, sir, they are not. I think it is best if you have as little contact as possible, for now. I will relay the message. Be safe, sir." And with that Mr. Chance hung up the phone and came back into the room.

"Hey, Mr. Chance, who was that?" Tom asked eagerly.

"That was a private phone call. You should not have

been eavesdropping," Mr. Chance scolded.

"Sorry, it's a small place!" Tom said, defending himself.

"Was it someone involved in our mission? Was it someone from R.O.N.I.N.?" Mitch joined in.

"Yes, it was a call regarding the mission. That is all I will say on the matter. Rest assured, everything will become clear in due time." The boys knew it was no use—the conversation about the phone call was over.

Mitch cleared his throat. "Maybe now's the time to tell us what that mission is, Mr. Chance."

Mr. Chance nodded and handed each of them a cup of tea. "The Rogue Operative Network has monitored the situation here in Japan for many decades. Recently our agents have discovered evidence that a terrorist attack is imminent."

"Evidence?" Mitch said. "What kind of evidence?"

"Why, I've already given you copies of the evidence," replied Mr. Chance, feigning surprise.

Tom snapped his fingers. "The manga!"

"You mean that stupid comic book?" Laura said incredulously. "You're telling us we've traveled halfway around the world because of a manga published by some corporation?"

Mr. Chance folded his hands behind his back. "Technically it's not a manga, but a *doujinshi*. And Matsu

Cybernetics had nothing to do with its publication."

"Huh?" Tom asked, confused.

"A *doujinshi* is a comic book featuring a popular character," Mr. Chance explained. "In this case it's Matsuki, the mascot of the Matsu School. But a *doujinshi* is written and drawn by fans, not by the people who own the character."

"Can't you get sued for that?" asked Mitch.

Mr. Chance nodded. "In America and Europe, yes. But in Japan, fan fiction about your character is considered flattery. The creators are honored to have their characters live on through the imaginations of their fans."

Tom considered the man's words. "I looked through the pictures," he said. "Matsuki saves Japan from a volcanic eruption . . . at least that's what I think happens."

"You are correct about the plot, but there is more to the story," said Mr. Chance. "The book I gave you was published just last week. According to the story, an evil outsider takes control of Matsu Cybernetics. Then he builds a device that will cause Mount Fuji to erupt and destroy much of Japan."

"So what's the big deal?" Tom said. "It's just a story, right?"

"A very curious story," noted Mr. Chance. "Curious because Matsu Cybernetics has built a secret research center at the base of Mount Fuji. Curious because the *doujinshi* features as its villain an international businessman named Jueru Kyogi."

"Yeah, I remember him. He's the masked dude with the cape," said Mitch. "But what's a fictional villain got to do with anything?"

"Most curious, this villain's name," Mr. Chance explained. "*Jueru* is a Japanese word for jewel. And the English translation for *kyogi* is vanity, or vain."

"So the name translates to Jewel Vanity," Tom said. "So what?"

Mitch elbowed his brother. "That sounds an awful lot like *Julian Vane*, don't you think?"

Tom's mouth gaped when he heard the name, and Laura gasped—with good reason. Julian Vane was the ruthless international financier and a traitor to Laura's father. Vane was also the leader of an evil group of Black Lotus ninjas. He and his ninjas had terrorized Laura's mother and brothers and destroyed their Chinatown computer store.

"I am convinced the similarity in names is more than coincidence," Mr. Chance told them. "Especially since after Mr. Vane fled New York City, R.O.N.I.N. operatives tracked him down in Japan. He has since dropped off the radar yet again."

"Do you think he's somehow connected to Matsu Cybernetics?" Mitch asked.

"We cannot be sure until the author of this manga is found and reveals what he knows," said Mr. Chance.

"So who's the author?" asked Laura.

"The name on the manga is Tanukis," noted Mr. Chance. "Coincidentally, there was also a student named Kim Tanukis enrolled at the Matsu School. She is a thirteen-year-old orphan from Yokohama. Until recently she lived with her elderly aunt."

"What happened?" Tom asked.

"She vanished, along with her aunt," said Mr. Chance. "Their apartment is abandoned."

Mitch frowned. "I guess if Kim revealed one of Julian Vane's secret plots, then she had good reason to disappear–"

"Or she *got disappeared*," Tom interrupted, "if you get my meaning."

"Whatever the case, it is clear that something is rotten at the Matsu School," Mr. Chance said. "Your mission is to find out what happened to young Kim and learn if there is any truth to her most curious comic book."

Tom, Laura, and Mitch exchanged uneasy glances.

"You may face danger, so you must proceed with caution," said Mr. Chance. After a pause, he added, "I certainly don't want any of *you* to end up *disappeared*."

CHAPTER 2

7:40 A.M. THE MATSU SCHOOL

The elevator traveled so fast that Mitch, Laura, and Tom felt as though they'd climbed aboard an invisible rocket. The car ran up the outside of the Matsu Cybernetics Tower. Through its transparent glass floor, the kids watched the streets of central Tokyo fall away with disturbing speed.

"This is one radical ride to school!" Tom cried, feeling exhilarated.

"Right," said Mitch, swallowing down his breakfast. "Radical."

"Aw, c'mon!" Tom grinned. "Don't tell me you're not loving this."

"I'm not loving this," Mitch answered, convinced that his stomach had just dropped to his heels. "I'm not loving anything that rearranges my anatomy."

"Well, I'll take a rocket to the clouds over a slow school bus any day!" said Tom.

"Not me," Laura said, her back pressed against the elevator doors. "I hate heights."

"Then you better not look down," advised Mitch.

"Or forward, or up," Tom added. "Actually, we're surrounded by glass, so you better just close your eyes."

Laura moaned. "I don't feel so good."

"Try to hold down breakfast a little longer," Mitch told her, swallowing hard again himself. "We're almost at the top."

A moment later the car slowed, then stopped. With a quiet hiss the doors slid aside, revealing the Matsu School's solarium—a spacious, glass-enclosed deck suspended high above the city streets. Laura stepped across the threshold, happy to finally have a visible means of support under her feet.

Voices and footsteps echoed inside the massive space, which was crowded with scores of kids in Matsu's formal uniforms—boys in black suits, girls in gray skirts and jackets.

The area reminded Tom of a rowdy mall, with food kiosks and benches scattered around. He also saw skateboard ramps, a rock-climbing wall, video games, and even—bizarrely—a bowling alley.

While Tom was checking out the activities, Mitch was studying the people. He immediately noticed that not every student was alike, despite their identical uniforms.

While most were Japanese, there were also kids from India, Africa, Europe—seemingly every continent in the world.

Some students wore items of traditional clothing from their native country. Mitch spotted girls from India and the Middle East with saris or burkas over their uniforms, and guys from India and Saudi Arabia wearing turbans or kaffiyehs.

A bunch of howling dudes raced by on skateboards. Tom whistled, impressed with their speed and flash. He tried to talk to one of them, but the guy ignored him. In fact, no one offered the newcomers a second glance.

"Not too friendly around here," Tom noted.

"It's a big place," Mitch replied. "They probably don't know we're new here."

"It's almost time for class," said Laura. "But we still don't know where to go or who to report to."

"The brochure said to check an information station. There's one over there," Mitch said, pointing.

The three of them approached the monitor, which resembled an ATM machine back home. Together they read the instructions, which flashed across the screen in English, Chinese, French, Farsi, German, and Japanese.

Using the keypad, Tom punched in his name. The results appeared within a second.

"It seems my first class is Graphic Design in room 310. Four hours of study, then a lunch break at noon."

Laura entered her name next.

"I'm going to room 324," she announced. "Designing Virtual Realities. I have lunch at noon too."

"Great," said Mitch, typing his own name into the computer. "Let's meet at that noodle shop over there at twelve o'clock. We can . . ." As Mitch's voice trailed off, he blinked in surprise.

"What's the matter, dude?" Tom asked.

"I'm going to room 101," he replied.

"What's the name of the class?" Laura asked.

"More important, when's your lunch?" asked Tom.

"I don't know," Mitch said, confused. "All it says is to report to room 101."

They stood in silence for a moment. Around them, the other students began to move toward the elevators and escalators.

Tom glanced at his watch. "Almost eight o'clock. Time for our first class."

"I'd better run," Laura said. "I don't even know where room 324 is yet!"

"It's probably three floors up," Tom told her. "Anyway, the escalators are over there."

"Right," said Laura. "See you at noon, I guess."

"Good luck, you guys," Tom called over his shoulder before vanishing into the crowd.

Mitch scratched his head, still confused by the lack

of information on his own schedule. Then he plowed ahead, in search of room 101.

He walked by many classrooms on the way, each a citadel of technology featuring high-definition screens for blackboards and an ultrasophisticated computer at every desk.

Because Mitch had registered for advanced computer science, he couldn't wait to see his own classroom. Then he found room 101. For a minute, he thought he'd come to the wrong place.

The chamber was tiny, not much larger than a walk-in storage closet. The walls were painted a dingy white and unadorned. The only furniture was a long workbench and three chairs. Three ten-inch computer monitors sat on the workbench, screens dark. Mitch saw wires dangling from the rear panels and realized they weren't connected to anything.

Beside each monitor sat a small aluminum box. Mitch tried to open one, but it was locked tight. He couldn't even find the handle. Weirdest of all, the back of the classroom was nothing more than a computer junkyard.

Electronics debris of all kinds was heaped from floor to ceiling. There were wires, microchips, keypads, motherboards, processors, and hard drives.

Mitch glanced at his wristwatch. One minute to eight o'clock and no sign of the teacher. He was about to walk away, convinced his assignment to room 101 had been some kind of mistake, when two students entered and calmly sat down.

Mitch guessed that both guys were about his age. One was Japanese, somewhat pudgy, with a thick neck. The other boy was dark-eyed and thin. He wore a turban, so Mitch guessed he was from India.

He was about to call out a greeting when he remembered rule number one from the Matsu School orientation guide—no talking in the classroom.

Speaking with friends was permitted in the solarium, at the food stands, and even in the halls between classes, but it was never allowed in the classroom.

Tight-lipped, Mitch offered the newcomers a silent nod. The Japanese kid grinned in return. The Indian boy seemed nervous and looked away.

A buzzer rang, signaling the start of class. Mitch sat down between the other two and stared at his blank monitor screen, waiting in silence for the lessons to begin.

A minute passed. Then two. Suddenly the sound of an electronically altered voice filled the room. The sound seemed to come from everywhere. Mitch looked for speakers, but saw none.

"In the next four hours you must each build a computer using only the parts and tools inside this room," the voice announced.

Mitch heard a click. The aluminum box next to his arm opened automatically, revealing a set of tools.

"Your computer must be capable of running the program contained on the memory stick inside your box. You may begin at any time," the voice continued.

Mitch looked over his shoulder at the sorry pile of junk behind him, wondering if accomplishing his assignment was possible.

"Remember. We will be watching you," the voice said ominously.

CHAPTER 3

ROOM 324, THE MATSU SCHOOL

Static flickered across the high-definition screen at the front of the classroom. In a burst of light and color, a short animated film appeared, starring the school mascot, Matsuki.

A member of the class had generated the digital program on a personal computer. The artist herself stood at attention beside her desk, eyes downcast, while Miss Nikki coolly evaluated her work in front of the class.

"The central figure moves very stiffly, and these poses are most unnatural," the young teacher declared. "Your colors clash and the overall effect is unattractive."

Laura Ting winced in sympathy. This was the fifth student whose work had been dissected by their teacher. Laura didn't think the short animation was so bad. In fact, she thought that the teacher could have said a lot of encouraging things while still being critical. Apparently that wasn't Miss Nikki's style.

"Most displeasing is the background. The sky seems dull, not luminous, and the clouds look like wrinkled futons." Miss Nikki shook her head and stared down at the girl. "Your overall performance has been mediocre. Unless your work improves, there will be no place for you in this class."

Way harsh, thought Laura. If that were me, I'd give it right back to her.

Instead the student bowed respectfully. "Thank you, Miss Nikki," she said softly, then quickly took her seat again.

Laura knew her own digital creation was no better than the one being reviewed. With a sinking feeling, she realized she was destined to experience the same hurtful evaluation.

Well, Mr. Chance, you can't accuse me of not fitting in, she mused. Miss Nikki hasn't said one nice thing about anybody's work yet!

The seventeen-year-old teacher was only a couple of years older than her students, with straight black hair and bangs that nearly covered her eyes. She wore the same uniform as the Matsu female students too, but the young teacher radiated the confidence and authority of someone far older.

Laura knew from paging through the school guidebook that there were many student teachers at the

Matsu School. Gifted upperclassmen and -women who excelled at a particular subject were selected by the faculty to teach first-year students. To Laura, however, all Miss Nikki appeared to be teaching was Nastiness for Beginners.

As the young teacher approached another student, Laura held her breath. The boy stood at attention when she reached his desk. Miss Nikki touched a button on the keypad, and the boy's digital animation appeared on the screen.

"Most disappointing," Miss Nikki said, shaking her head.

While the teacher launched into another savage critique, Laura's attention was drawn to the girl beside her—or rather, to the image on that girl's monitor. The animated scene featured a flying Matsuki. What impressed Laura were the details: the determined expression on the creature's face, and the way its ears blew back against the wind as it raced through the air at top speed.

The other girl noticed Laura's stare. Her name was Emiko, and she had long, dark hair with pink streaks. She smiled at Laura, shyly hiding her mouth behind her hand. Laura spied a flash of silver and recalled the humiliating year she herself had spent wearing braces.

Emiko swiveled her monitor so Laura could get a better

look at her work, then pressed a button. Laura nearly gasped when the flying Matsuki figure morphed into a beautiful, multicolored floating dragon. The creature had glowing green eyes and digital scales that rippled in flight. The image was detailed to seemingly jump out of the screen.

"This is how you waste your time, Emiko?"

The voice was sharp and nasty. Emiko literally jumped out of her seat when she saw Miss Nikki standing over her.

"With respect, teacher, I have followed the lesson to the best of my ability." Emiko bowed. "Please let me start the animation from the beginning and—"

The young teacher folded her arms. "You were to animate the school mascot, were you not?"

"Yes, Miss Nikki. And I have. If you let me start the program from the beginning, you will see—"

But Miss Nikki ignored Emiko's words. She punched the delete button on the girl's keypad and the wondrous image faded away as the monitor went black.

"You will return this afternoon after regular classes and repeat the required assignment before you progress to the next lesson," Miss Nikki commanded.

Emiko bowed again. "Yes. Thank you, Miss Nikki."

Then Miss Nikki leveled her cold gaze on Laura. "Let us see what our newest student has created."

Laura stood at attention. Miss Nikki touched the

keypad and Laura's digital creation flashed on the big screen.

Miss Nikki gazed at the image and sighed. "Are you sure you are in the right class, Laura Ting?"

Oh, I'm in the right class, all right, Laura raged inwardly. And this is the right time to tell you exactly what a nasty witch of a teacher you are.

Laura opened her mouth, then shut it again. She could almost hear Mr. Chance in her head. You're here to find Kim Tanukis and solve the riddle of the bizarre comic, not flunk out on the very first day!

Laura knew she had to play along, even if it meant swallowing her pride.

"Yes, Miss Nikki," Laura replied meekly, eyes downcast. But at her sides, Laura clenched her fists until her knuckles turned white.

侍

Meanwhile, in room 101, Mitch quickly determined that the computer parts piled up around him were far from junk. The room was sheer chaos, with boards and processors stacked everywhere, but among the debris he saw enough solid components to build a dozen computers.

While some of the equipment was obsolete, a lot of it was cutting-edge, fresh from the manufacturer, and Mitch decided there was more to this test than building a basic computer out of scraps. As he saw it, the real test would be to build the very *best* computer possible with the components available. That meant he had to make smart, careful choices and not grab just anything.

Alongside the other boys, Mitch began rummaging through the equipment. It took some time, but he carefully selected the most powerful processor, the best memory storage system, the fastest microchips, the most efficient motherboard.

Sometimes he had to compromise. Not every system was compatible, and Mitch found himself sacrificing speed for efficiency. But when he finally dragged his parts to the workbench, he was satisfied with the choices he'd made.

With the meager tools at hand, Mitch began to assemble his machine. Lost in concentration, he forgot the time. As the hours flew by, he loaded the test program and ran it several times.

A loud buzzer jolted him back to reality. "The assignment has ended," the disembodied voice announced. "Please return your tools to the box and break for lunch. Return here at two o'clock for an evaluation of your work."

侍

Tom walked into the solarium and headed for the crowded noodle stand. He looked around for Laura and Mitch, but neither one had arrived yet, so he found an empty table beside the tall windows and sat down.

On the other side of the glass, the pinnacles of the city's skyscrapers sparkled in the noonday sun. Though the view was spectacular, Tom's eyes were drawn back inside to a group of boys weaving through the lunchtime crowd on skateboards. He was impressed by their speed and control, amazed they didn't run anyone over. The leader of the pack was a tall Japanese kid riding a board emblazoned with a scarlet lightning bolt.

Mitch appeared, and Tom waved him over. "So how did things go in the mysterious room 101?" Tom asked.

"It was the weirdest class I've ever had," Mitch told him, sitting down at the table. "No teacher, just a voice, and the class *started* with an exam."

"Whoa!" Tom shuddered.

"Nothing I couldn't handle," said Mitch with a confident wave of his hand. "How about you?"

Tom shrugged. "My teacher's a young guy named Tomo. I understood about half of what he said, and that's only thanks to you."

"It's kind of loud in here. Could you repeat that?" Mitch said, cupping his ear. "I didn't hear you right because I thought you said 'thank you.'"

"Ha, ha. Very funny."

Mitch looked around. "Seriously. Why is it so noisy in here?"

Tom shrugged. "I guess the students make up for silent classes by screaming their heads off at lunch."

Mitch sniffed the savory aromas coming from the food stand, then glanced at his watch. "Speaking of lunch, Laura's late and I'm hungry."

Tom tore his eyes away from the frenetic skateboarders. "Then let's get in line, bro. It's a long one, and Laura will probably show up before we place our order."

Mitch led the way and Tom followed. As the brothers moved toward the food line, the boys on skateboards zoomed right in front of Tom, cutting him off from following Mitch.

Forced to stop short, Tom waited for the parade of skateboarders to pass. Meanwhile, Mitch kept walking toward the food stand.

"Yo, Mitch! Wait up," Tom yelled. But his brother continued walking until he melted into the crowd.

Tom scanned the solarium, looking for his brother. He was so intent on locating Mitch that he didn't notice the grinning skateboarder careening right for him at top speed.

CHAPTER 4

LEVEL THREE, THE MATSU SCHOOL

Laura caught up with Emiko in the hallway after class.

"Hi," she said. "My name's Laura Ting, and I just wanted to say I'm sorry our psycho teacher deleted your animated dragon. I thought your work was amazing."

"I am Emiko Gensai, but please call me Emi," the other girl replied. "And his name is Tenchouchikyuu-Doragon."

Laura blinked. "Excuse me?"

"What you call the dragon. The creature I created," said Emiko. "It's a *kami*—a spirit—much celebrated by the folks in my hometown. Tenchouchikyuu-Doragon," she repeated. "His name means 'Dragon of Heaven and Earth.'"

"Where's your hometown?" Laura asked.

"Outside of Tokyo. Just a train ride away," said Emiko. "You're from America, right?"

Laura nodded. "New York City."

Emiko's eyes went wide. "Wow! I want to live in New York someday. I want to go to the museums and visit Yoko Ono at her Central Park mansion. I want to be NEET."

"Neat?" Laura laughed. "I think you meant to say cool, right? Or fly or phat? Neat is kind of old slang—"

"Not that kind of neat," Emiko said with a wave of her hand. "NEETs are what we call young people who move to New York City to study art. It means 'Not in Education, Employment, or Training.'"

"Sounds kind of like an insult," Laura said.

"It is, but we bohemians do not care. Art is all that matters," replied Emiko.

"Well, you're a great artist. Doragon is quite beautiful—*was* quite beautiful, I mean."

Emiko touched the small, teardrop-shaped crystal that dangled from a silver chain around her neck. She unfastened the clasp and handed the necklace to Laura.

"Here," she said. "Since you like it so much, it is yours to keep."

Confused, Laura took the crystal, then realized the gem was really a tiny portable memory drive.

"Cool!" she exclaimed. "I mean, thank you." She gave Emiko a little bow. "I'll download the program into my computer and return the necklace to you."

"Please keep them both," Emiko told her. "Consider it a 'welcome to our school' present. I doubt anyone else here will offer you one."

Laura frowned. "Yeah. Even the teachers are unfriendly."

"Not all of them. Miss Nikki is . . . special."

With Emiko's help, Laura placed the necklace around her own throat. She thanked Emiko again.

"I came here to study art and computer graphics," said Laura.

"That's my major too," Emiko replied. "To study here is my dream."

"I came to the Matsu School because I was impressed by the art created by one of the students here," Laura went on. "Maybe you know her. Her name is Kim Tanukis."

Emiko shook her head. "Sorry, I don't. But Matsu School is a big place."

"Her work is very special," Laura said. "Maybe Kim is one of the student teachers, like Miss Nikki."

Emiko frowned. "There are no student teachers as special as Miss Nikki. Nikki Matsu is the daughter of Mr. Inoshiro Matsu, the founder and CEO of Matsu

Cybernetics. He's the big boss of this school."

It took Laura a moment to get over her surprise and process that information.

"Do not fret," Emiko continued. "There are always ways to hook up with other students."

"Oh yeah?" Laura asked, interested.

"Most everyone has a Matsukuwa," Emiko said, reaching into her bag.

Laura stared blankly. "A what?"

"It's a play on words," Emiko explained. "Matsuki is the school mascot, of course, and *zokuwa* means gossip. Here!"

Emiko displayed what looked like a toy cell phone. The case was yellow plastic molded in the cute shape of Matsuki.

"A cell phone?"

"It's a pocket bell," Emiko replied. "A type of telephone that uses a special frequency that allows them to broadcast only to owners of the same device. Only kids from the Matsu School can own a Matsukuwa."

"Where can I get one of these?" Laura asked.

"There is a shop in the solarium," said Emiko. "Come. I'll take you there now. Then, tonight, we'll go to Shibuya District and look for this mysterious Kim Tanukis together."

"I don't understand," replied Laura.

Emiko laughed. "Don't worry. I'll explain everything to my new friend from New York City."

侍

Tom grunted when he hit the floor, the wind knocked out of him. Through bleary eyes he looked up to see that dozens of students had formed a tight circle around him. They wore expressions of shock, horror, and even pity. But none of them moved to help him.

Meanwhile, the guy who'd struck Tom down turned inside the circle and rolled toward him. Tom sat up just as the kid skidded to a halt beside him. In one swift move, he stepped off the back of the board, flipped it into the air with his foot, and caught it with one hand.

That's when Tom saw the lightning bolt on the board and realized he'd collided with the leader of the pack. The leader also had a lightning bolt tattooed over his left eyebrow.

Tom heard the onlookers whispering. Then someone called out the kid's name.

"Kunio!"

"So sorry, Gai-jin," Kunio said, smirking.

Tom didn't know what *Gai-jin* meant, but from the expression on the kid's face, he guessed it was an insult. But then Kunio surprised him by extending his hand. Tom grabbed it and Kunio hauled him to his feet.

"Thanks," said Tom, dusting himself off. "My name is—"

"HAH!"

Kunio kicked out and spun, cutting Tom's legs out from under him. Feet in the air, Tom landed on his backside so hard that he bit his tongue. He tasted blood.

Some of Kunio's friends appeared. They chuckled while they circled Tom on their boards. No one else made a sound.

Kunio loomed over him. "Just having a little fun, new boy. Come on, up you go."

Once again, Kunio extended his hand. Once again, he wore the same smirk. Tom grasped the hand again. But as Kunio yanked him to his feet, Tom felt the other kid's muscles tense and knew Kunio was up to his old tricks.

"HAH!"

Kunio's cry was accompanied by the same spin-and-trip move he'd pulled the last time. But Tom was ready. With his left arm, he deflected the kick. Still clutching Kunio's hand, Tom rolled onto his back, dragging the other kid down with him. As Tom tumbled, he used his legs to flip his opponent over his head.

Kunio slammed into a pair of his friends, and the three of them crashed to the floor. For the first time since the collision, Tom heard from the crowd. The onlookers began to laugh. Some of them even applauded.

His face flushed with anger and embarrassment, Kunio leaped to his feet. His two friends rose as well. Meanwhile, Tom dropped into a crouch, arms raised. He watched warily as the trio stalked him.

Finally one kid lurched forward—only to be knocked flat by a straight-arm block to the throat. The crowd parted again and Mitch stepped forward.

"Whoa, guys," he declared. "My brother Tom can eat a lot of noodles, but don't worry. I'm sure there's enough ramen for everybody!"

Kunio sneered and faced the newcomer.

"Your argument's with me," Tom snarled. "Leave my brother out of this."

Alarm bells rang. Red lights flashed. With startled cries, the kids fled the scene.

"Stop fighting at once or you will all be expelled." The disembodied voice echoed throughout the entire solarium, in a tone that was both commanding and ominously calm.

Kunio lowered his arms immediately, before lifting his eyes skyward. Tom looked up too and saw a shiny metal globe with lenses for eyes hovering near the glass ceiling.

"Who is responsible for this altercation?" demanded the voice.

"No one, sir. There was no altercation," Kunio replied smoothly. "I was merely demonstrating my skateboarding skills to the new student from America."

Eyes staring from under his bangs, Kunio challenged Tom to dispute his version of events. Tom opened his mouth to speak, then thought better of it. According to the school guidebook, a fight resulted in instant expulsion for both students, no matter who started it.

"That's right, sir," Tom said. "Kunio here lost his balance. He's really kind of a klutz."

"Return to your studies," the voice said after a pause. Tom watched the metal sphere drift away to another part of the solarium.

Kunio bent down to retrieve his board and tucked it under his arm. Tom turned his back on him and walked to his brother.

"Yo, Gai-jin."

Tom whirled to face Kunio. The Japanese kid made a fist, thumb pointing upward. "Next time," he said. Slowly Kunio turned his hand until his thumb was pointing at the floor.

His gang surrounded him. Without another glance, Kunio walked away.

Mitch touched Tom's arm. "Dude, are you okay?"

Tom stared at Kunio's back. "I'm okay, but I'm getting tired of people attacking me for no reason!"

Mitch scanned the faces of the kids around them. "Well, he has everyone else around here running scared, so he's either the school bully, or—"

"Or someone who's seen *Gladiator* one too many times," Tom interrupted. "Either way, he's trouble."

"You're both right," a voice behind them remarked. "Kunio *is* the school bully, and you two are in a lot of trouble for standing up to him."

CHAPTER 5

SOLARIUM, THE MATSU SCHOOL

Tom and Mitch spun around to face the boy who'd spoken. He had a crew cut and was a little overweight. Mitch recognized the kid immediately.

"You're from my class," he said, relieved.

"Brian Saito, at your service," the boy said, with a slight bow.

"I'm Mitch Hearn and this is my brother Tom."

"Wow! You're really brothers?" Brian folded his arms and smiled. "I never would have guessed."

Tom's eyes narrowed. He looked about ready to blow. Mitch quickly put a hand over Tom's mouth.

"If you want to stick around," he calmly warned Brian, "the twin jokes stop now."

Brian shrugged. "Deal."

Tom pushed Mitch's hand away from his face and glanced over his shoulder. "I'm a reasonable guy, but

right now I want to knock that smirk off Kunio's face. Way off . . ."

"That would be dumb," Brian advised. "Kunio and his gang pretty much run things around here. Kids who stand up to them don't last long. The all-seeing Eyes in the Sky have been known to miss a trick or two. Sometimes people get hurt, and nobody knows how."

Mitch frowned. "'Eyes in the Sky'? What's that?"

"That floating metal globe that broke up the fight," said Brian. "You'll find them all over the place, if you look—hovering in the halls and classrooms, the cafeteria. I've heard they can do more than spy, too, but that may just be a rumor."

"What do you mean?" Tom's brow wrinkled. "Are you talking killer robot sentinels?"

"This *is* Tokyo, Gai-jin," Brian reminded him. "It's all computers and robots at Matsu. It's the Eyes that keep order around here. Matsu School is their world; we just live in it."

"Their world—or Kunio's?" asked Tom.

Brian arched an eyebrow. "Good point."

"Dude, you're cold, and way too cynical," Mitch told Brian.

"Call me a realist," Brian replied. "I'm just trying to stay out of trouble, you know?"

"Are you from Tokyo?" asked Mitch.

Brian shook his head. "Tacoma, Washington. But I hardly remember the place. I'm what they call a navy brat. I've lived in ten places in thirteen years. Then I came to Matsu School and found a home. This is my second year."

"You *like* it here?" Tom asked, surprised.

"It's the best game in town," said Brian. "I came because Matsu offered a better education than Microsoft's or Apple's mentoring programs. To be the best, you've got to study with the best."

"And I thought Mitch was a brainiac," Tom said, groaning.

"All I'm saying is you've got to start early with a quality education if you want to make the big bucks," Brian replied.

"Is that all you want to do? Make big bucks?" asked Mitch.

Brian seemed surprised at the question. "Sure, dude. Don't you?"

Mitch smiled. "Actually, I want lunch. How about you two?"

Brian patted his belly. "I didn't attain this gut through lack of exercise alone. Lead on, Gai-jin," he told Mitch.

"Dude, what does Gai-jin mean, exactly?" Tom asked as they walked toward the noodle stand.

Brian smiled. "You don't want to know."

侍

When the five o'clock bell rang, the disembodied voice dismissed Mitch and Brian. Silently, the two rose from their workbenches and filed out of room 101. As soon as they reached the hallway, they cheered and high-fived each other.

"I can't believe it," Mitch cried, shaking his head.

"Believe it," Brian replied. "We passed the entrance exam! Now I'm finally in Matsu's advanced program! And so are you."

As Brian spoke, the two negotiated the crowded hallway and reached the escalators.

"Too bad about the other kid," Mitch said.

Brian shrugged. "He'll get another shot next semester." Then a grin crossed his round face. "Looks like the third time was the charm for me."

Mitch blinked. "So you've been in room 101 before?"

"I took the test on my very first day at Matsu School—just like you," Brian told him. "I was called back at the beginning of last semester. I failed both times . . . but not today!"

Mitch scratched his head. "So what now?"

"Now nothing's going to be the same! We're in the program, dude! This is the opportunity of a lifetime."

Mitch shrugged. "I've taken advanced courses before. A class is just a class, right?"

"Not here. For a couple of weeks we'll go to a few special classes. But after that, things get real serious really fast. You'll be taken out of the school and put to work in the corporate labs—"

"Whoa!"

"My thought exactly," said Brian. "You'll learn computer technology from researchers and software engineers, not teachers. Even better, advanced students move into the dormitory—"

"Dormitory?"

Brian paused, scanned the crowded halls around them, then glanced upward. Mitch got the uneasy feeling that his classmate was checking to see if an Eye was hovering nearby.

"There's a dormitory somewhere inside this building,"

Brian whispered. "That's where all the true geniuses study. With luck, we'll be living there real soon. Maybe we'll even be roommates."

Mitch frowned. While the thought of working in the labs excited him, everything else Brian said about the advanced program made him uneasy.

"It'll be weird not having Tom around all the time," Mitch said, "but I guess I'll see my brother at lunchtime, or after school when we hang out."

Brian shook his head. "Advanced students don't have time to hang out, man. They're too cool for school. They're either working in the labs or studying in the dorm. It's like computer heaven."

"Sounds more like computer prison," said Mitch. "I'm going to miss my brother. Aren't you going to miss your family?"

Brian snorted. "What family? My parents are divorced. Mom lives with her new boyfriend in Hawaii. Dad flies jets for the U.S. Navy, so he's off on an aircraft carrier ten months out of the year. If Matsu Cybernetics wants to adopt me as a member of their corporate family, that's fine with me. Nothing wrong with trading up, right?"

Mitch didn't feel that way at all. His brother could be a pain sometimes, but he couldn't imagine life without him. It was already hard enough without his dad. And

Mr. Chance was like family—Mitch wouldn't "trade up" his soft-spoken guardian for anything.

As they went down the escalators, Mitch scanned the crowd in the solarium. He quickly found his brother sitting outside the noodle shop with Laura Ting and a Japanese girl.

"Come on," he told Brian, and they joined Tom and Laura, who introduced them to her new friend, Emiko.

While Tom and Laura talked about their day, Brian sidled up to Emiko and smiled.

"I've seen you around," he told her smoothly, "and I've always wondered why a girl as cool as you wasn't in any of my classes."

"Maybe you take boring classes," she replied.

Despite the afternoon sunlight pouring through the windows, everyone felt the chill—everyone but Brian, who seemed completely oblivious to Emiko's reaction.

"No more boring classes for me!" Brian declared, puffing out his chest. "I'm entering the advanced program."

"Wow, that *so* does not impress me in the slightest," said Emiko.

She turned her back on Brian and faced Laura. "I'm sorry, but I've got to go back to Miss Nikki's class and repeat this morning's lesson. Let's meet in front of the coffee shop at Center Gai at eight o'clock. I'll wait for you under the big TV screen."

Laura nodded. "Sounds good. I've got the directions."

"Wait a sec!" Mitch protested. "You're not going out on the town without Tom and me as your chaperones."

Laura smirked and folded her arms. "Wanna bet?"

"Hmm," said Brian. "The ladies are going to Shibuya, and they don't want chaperones? Sounds like they're up to no good."

Emiko tossed her pink locks. "That's right," she said coyly. "Tonight Laura and I are going to look for a very cool and very special someone."

Brian elbowed Mitch. "Guess I better be there, then. I wouldn't want to disappoint them."

Emiko rolled her eyes, then stood up. "Nice to meet you Tom, Mitch!" she called over her shoulder as she walked away.

"Hey, what about me?" yelled Brian. "Aren't you happy you met me, too?"

Emiko pretended not to hear as she hurried off.

"Did you see the way she acted?" Brian cried excitedly. "She really liked me. I could see it in her eyes!"

"Dude," Tom said, putting a hand on his shoulder, "I think you might need glasses."

CHAPTER 6

MATSU CYBERNETICS TOWER

Nikki Matsu squeezed through the elevator doors and pressed the button for the fiftieth floor.

When the young teacher had been called to her father's office, she'd dropped everything, left her classroom, and hurried to the teachers' lounge, where she used a special keycard to activate this secret elevator.

Before the doors even opened completely on the executive floor, Nikki raced through them. She stepped quickly through the waiting room, ignoring the spectacular view of Tokyo under a setting sun. Running by the secretary's desk, she scattered a swarm of shiny steel Eyes. Finally, without knocking, Nikki barged into the private office of Inoshiro Matsu, the founder and chief executive officer of Matsu Cybernetics.

As she suspected, Nikki found only an empty office chair and a high-definition monitor in the middle of her father's desk. Her cousin Kunio sat in a chair opposite the desk, facing the blank screen. He rose to greet her.

"I'm sorry to say that your father is not here, Nikki-*san*," Kunio said, bowing. "This is a video conference with Uncle Matsu."

Without comment Nikki sat down in a chair, arranged her uniform, and faced the screen, her tiny hands folded in her lap.

She noticed something different in her father's office. A shiny new computer station—a component of Matsu's newest mainframe computer—had been set up beside her father's expansive oaken desk. Nikki wondered why the control unit was here, since her father was not around to use it.

Her thoughts were interrupted when a digital picture appeared on one of the screens. Nikki smiled when she saw the familiar face of her father, despite her suspicions. He was in the family home in Honolulu, lounging in his favorite chair. Behind her father, the windows were open and the palm trees waved in the sun. Across a stretch of sand, Nikki could see the ocean waves pounding the shore.

The home was exactly as she remembered it, though she hadn't spent time there in several years.

Mr. Matsu brightened when he saw his daughter. "Nikki, you are well?" he asked.

From her chair, Nikki bowed her head respectfully. "I am very well, Father."

"And you, Kunio?" Mr. Matsu asked.

The boy nodded. "I am fine, Uncle. Work progresses on those special projects you assigned to me last time. In fact, I can report success on several fronts. . . ."

While her father discussed business with Kunio, Nikki considered the digital picture on the screen. She contemplated the way the ocean breeze stirred her father's iron gray hair. She noted that he was wearing the yellow shirt she'd bought him for his last birthday.

A nice touch. Almost convincing, Nikki thought.

"Daughter," said Mr. Matsu, "there is a student who reported to you after school today."

"Yes," she replied with a nod. "The girl's name is Emiko Gensai."

"And is Emiko a good student?" her father asked.

"Emiko could be exceptional, if she applied herself," Nikki replied honestly. "Her technical skills are impressive, and she has the eye of a great artist. Unfortunately, she seldom performs well in class because she is constantly daydreaming."

Her father's face seemed to freeze for a moment—a delay in the signal? Then he fixed Nikki with a commanding stare. "Emiko will not be returning to Matsu School. You must purge all records of her

DEEP IN THE WOODS . . .

THE QUIET WAS BROKEN BY A TRIO OF HELICOPTERS.

time here from the school computers."

Nikki's eyes narrowed with suspicion, but she nodded meekly. "I will do as you ask, Father."

Mr. Matsu shifted his gaze to her cousin. "Kunio, I want you to continue to work on the new student. But under no circumstances are you to harm his twin brother. My associate Julian Vane wishes to deal with the boy named Mitchell in his own way."

Kunio bowed his head. "I will obey, Uncle."

"Always remain vigilant," Mr. Matsu said. "This is a delicate time. Within a few hours, the first part of our plan will commence. Then—"

"I miss you, Father! When will you return?" Nikki cried, interrupting the man. She followed the outburst with sobs. Through her tears, she studied the image on the screen.

She noticed a slight pause, as if there'd been a delay in the satellite signal. Then the picture became pixelated. Finally the image reformed, and Mr. Matsu faced his daughter.

"I hope to return soon," he said evenly. "But right now I am very busy. My new project with Julian Vane requires my constant attention."

Nikki frowned, then took the tissue Kunio handed her. Inside, her mind was racing.

It was the same answer he gave me during the last

video conference, Nikki thought. More than that, his cold and unemotional tone was exactly the same!

Finally her suspicions had been confirmed. Now Nikki understood why her father acted the way he did, why he'd been away for so long—and why he might never come back. But despite the fear that welled up inside of her, she knew she had to continue being careful.

"I am sorry for acting so emotionally, Father," Nikki said.

On the screen, the image of Mr. Matsu smiled. "I understand, my child. You may go, Nikki. We will speak again soon."

Nikki rose. As she walked slowly to the door, she listened to her father's instructions to Kunio. She was surprised to hear Emiko's name mentioned again, then shocked by what she heard next.

侍

Laura met her friend in front of the coffee shop promptly at eight—though "shop" was hardly the word, because the place was the size of Texas. Fortunately, her new friend's pink-colored hair made Emiko easy to spot, even among the mob of young people all around them.

Emiko smiled when she saw Laura. And her smile widened even more at the sight of the teardrop-shaped crystal that Laura wore around her neck. She was happy that Laura was still wearing the gift she'd given her.

"You weren't kidding when you said the TV screen was big!" Laura exclaimed, amazed. "It's larger than my parents' store in Chinatown!"

Emiko laughed. "There are more two-story TV screens here than in any other district."

On the mammoth monitor above her head, Laura saw a scary-looking clown chasing a man in a cheesy duck suit. "I don't know if that's such a good thing," she commented, scratching her head at the ridiculous images.

"Come with me," Emiko told her.

"Are we going to look for Kim Tanukis?" asked Laura.

Emiko displayed her Matsukuwa. "I've put out the call," she said, shaking the phone. "Some of the other kids are looking for her now. We could have news any minute."

"Cool," Laura said.

Emiko led Laura to the "scramble crossing," a brilliantly illuminated, five-way intersection that was one of the most photographed spots in Tokyo. All around her, amid the blaring car horns and chattering crowds, Laura saw dazzling neon, animated signs, and giant TVs, some playing advertising loops over and over again.

Most amazing was the crowd. Except for the

shopkeepers and restaurant owners, there was almost no one older than twenty in this cool, cosmopolitan neighborhood.

"Shibuya is where all the teenagers in Tokyo come to hang out," Emiko explained.

They headed northeast, past the Hachiko exit of the Japanese Railroad's Shibuya station, where Emiko paused. "This is my favorite statue," she said.

Laura blinked. "Is that a dog? Who'd put up a statue of a dog?"

"Hachiko was a very special dog who is celebrated for his loyalty," Emiko explained. "Every morning Hachi accompanied his master to the train station, then returned in the evening to greet him when he arrived home."

"That's nice," said Laura, nodding.

"Hachi's loyalty continued beyond the grave," Emiko went on. "Even after his master was gone, the dog returned to the station each day to wait for him."

"Wow," Laura said. "That's so . . . *depressing*."

Emiko laughed. "You are right, and we are here to have fun—"

Just then the Matsukuwa buzzed in Emiko's pink

sequined purse. She answered, holding the phone so Laura could listen too.

"Hey, Emi! It's me, Brian Saito!" The voice quality on the tiny phone wasn't the best, but Laura recognized the voice of Mitch's new classmate in the advanced program.

Emiko obviously recognized him too. She frowned. "Oh, hello."

"Word's out you're looking for a girl named Kim Tanukis, right?" Brian continued.

Laura met Emiko's eyes and nodded vigorously.

"Yes, we're looking for her," Emiko admitted.

"Well," said Brian, "I'm on line at the Kup Kake Club and Kim is standing right in front of me!"

"I thought that place was closed," Emiko told him.

"They did close, for remodeling, but now they've opened again and it's cooler than ever. You should come over," Brian insisted.

Emiko covered the phone with her hand. "Do you want to go?" she asked.

"I'm not sure. I want to find Kim, but what's the Kup Kake Club?" Laura wondered.

"It's a sweet shop where kids hang out," explained Emiko. "It's really tiny, but très chic. It's in an alley off Koen-dori Street."

Laura looked around at the crowds and the tangle of traffic. "It's so busy around here, and Shibuya is so big," she said doubtfully. "What if we get separated?"

"Just call me on the Matsukuwa. And if you can't get a signal, then we'll agree to meet back here at Hachiko's statue," Emiko suggested.

Laura nodded. "Okay, that will work. Let's go find Kim!"

"We'll be there in thirty minutes. Tell Kim to stay and wait for us," Emiko told Brian before she hung up.

The pair crossed the street and moved through the crowded sidewalks of Koen-dori Street. They laughed and talked and window-shopped. Laura and Emiko were having so much fun that neither of them noticed two figures, swathed in black clothing, stalking them like silent ghosts.

CHAPTER 7

SHIBUYA DISTRICT, TOKYO, JAPAN

Mitch tugged on the sleeve of Tom's black sweatshirt. "Let's go, Pokey. The girls are on the move again."

Tom pulled his hood over his head to shield his face, adjusted the skateboard on his backpack, and then fell into lockstep beside his brother. The pair melted into the crowd flowing along the jam-packed sidewalks on Koen-dori Street.

"I thought you were crazy for stopping at that pet shop after school," Tom said. "But now I get it."

Mitch shook his head. "It's pathetic, really. You're always doubting my genius, and I'm always proving you wrong."

"Nobody loves an arrogant jerk. Especially not a geeky one," Tom replied.

Mitch sighed. "I just wish there was a cheaper way to keep tabs on Laura. This Pet Tracker cost a ton."

"Yeah, but it was worth every penny, dude," Tom assured his brother. "If you hadn't used that little device of yours, we would have lost them back at that crazy five-way intersection. How'd you know about it, anyway?"

"I read about it in a computer magazine," answered Mitch. "The homing device is small enough to fit into a dog or cat collar, so it was easy to slip it into Laura's Matsukuwa. Funny thing, though," he added, frowning. "When I opened the case, I discovered that the phone already had a tracking device built into it. If I knew the frequency, I could have homed in on that."

"Hmm," Tom said suspiciously. "I wonder if that's another way Matsu School keeps watch on its students when they're out of 'Eye' sight, if you know what I mean."

Mitch shrugged. "I know I'm not buying a Matsukuwa. I'm already feeling paranoid. . . . I keep feeling like *we're* being followed, but every time I turn around to look, no one's there."

Tom frowned. "You know what I think? I think you're not paranoid if they really *are* out to get you."

Mitch glanced at the tracker in his hand. "I hate it when you think. So stop doing it and watch the girls, because you are totally bumming me out."

"My eyes are on the prize," said Tom.

"Please don't let them see you," Mitch cautioned. "I'd hate for Laura to know we followed her."

"But we're doing it for her own good," Tom replied.

"I know that and you know that, but Laura might not see things quite the same way," Mitch said. "Better if we just stay out of sight so she never even knows we were here."

侍

Laura peered down the long, crooked alley. It was too narrow for cars to negotiate, even the tiny cars of Japan. The pavement was uneven, the darkness broken in patches only by dull electric lightbulbs disguised as paper lanterns.

"Are you sure this is the right place?" Laura asked doubtfully.

"Sure I'm sure," Emiko replied. "The Kup Kake Club is just around the corner. Come on."

Emiko charged forward, her stacked heels clicking on the pavement. Laura reluctantly followed. A few moments later they turned the corner. Ahead they saw a door, with a neon sign that said KUP KAKE. But the electric sign was dark, and when they tried the door, it was locked.

"Closed," Emiko said.

"I have a bad feeling about this," whispered Laura. "Let's get out of here."

"Which way do you want to go?" Emiko asked. "We can go right or left—there are some pretty phat clubs either way. Or we can go back to Koen-dori Street."

"Let's go back the way we came," Laura decided. "There are more people there."

Emiko nodded. "We're going. But first I'm going to give it to that jerk Brian for sending us here. I'm sure he's chuckling over his little prank right now."

Emiko pulled the Matsukuwa out of her purse and pressed redial. But before she could put the phone to her ear, a strange sound broke the stillness. "What's that?" she asked.

Laura tensed. "Engines. Wheels on pavement. And they're getting closer."

侍

"I can't believe you lost them," Tom groaned.

"They're close to where we're standing. Look, there's the blip, right here on the tracking screen," Mitch cried defensively.

Tom looked around. "Then why can't I see them?"

While Mitch fiddled with his device, Tom made a complete scan of the neighborhood. There were a few small shops, but all of them had big picture windows.

If Laura and Emiko were inside one of them, he would have seen them.

Out of the silence came a rustling sound, followed by the shuffling of footsteps. The boys stopped dead in their tracks and began to search for the source.

"Whoa! What's that?" cried Tom, as a figure clad in black darted around the bend. "Did you see that guy?"

"Do you think that guy was following us? I thought I was just being paranoid earlier, but this is getting ridiculous," Mitch replied.

"Mr. Chance told us to be cautious. There's a reason these missions are top secret and dangerous," Tom reminded his brother. "Let's just find Laura and Emiko and get out of here."

Then Tom spotted the alley, half-hidden by a sushi restaurant's sign. He tapped his brother's shoulder. Mitch glanced up, then back down at his tracking screen. "You found them," he said.

They moved down the alley until they saw a corner fifty yards ahead. Suddenly Tom stopped in his tracks.

"What's—"

Tom shushed his brother. He'd just heard a familiar sound—a noise that made the hair on the back of his neck stand up.

"Move!" Tom cried, shoving his brother against the wall.

Tom whirled to see three men in dark suits and sunglasses racing toward him.

He wasn't sure if they were coming for him, but after what they'd been through in the past few weeks, he wasn't taking any chances. "Bro, grab your skateboard," Tom cried, looking back at his brother. "It's time to book it. I don't know what these guys are after, but they don't look friendly. We might need a quick getaway."

The boys unstrapped their skateboards from their backpacks and started to run down the street as fast as they could. The suited men were gaining on them, and soon the boys came to the end of the street.

"Quick, down those stairs!" cried Tom.

"But what about Laura and Emiko?" asked Mitch, nervous they might lose the girls again.

"Dude, we're running for our lives here! We'll deal with the girls later," Tom insisted.

The brothers jetted down the stairs, hopping onto their skateboards when one of the men pulled out a long sword from behind his back. Suddenly they heard a loud crash; it sounded like something had just smashed into a pile of trash cans. The suited men halted their pursuit, but the boys kept on skating. As they darted past, they saw the darkly clothed guy from the street race past them in the opposite direction. When the boys turned around to check their backs, everyone had vanished.

"What was that?!" Tom cried, slowing down his board. "Why would they chase us for two blocks and then disappear?"

"Maybe they weren't actually chasing *us*," Mitch pointed out. "I think I may have twisted my ankle on those stairs."

"Let me see," Tom insisted, pushing hard on Mitch's left ankle.

"Ouch!" Mitch cried in pain. "Can we just rest for a minute?"

"Yeah, okay."

The boys put down their skateboards and leaned up against a wall to rest. Suddenly they heard a girl scream.

"You stay here. I'll go!" Tom cried.

"I'll catch up!" yelled Mitch.

Tom roared away while Mitch attempted to follow at a manageable pace.

侍

The skateboarders came from every direction at once. Dozens of them.

Roaring down the alley, the gang quickly circled Emiko and Laura, corralling them. Silently they circled the pair like hungry vultures.

"Stay away, you creeps!" Emiko warned. "I have Mace!"

She paused to fumble in her purse.

"No!" cried Laura, trying to keep the girl at her side. Suddenly one of the boarders darted from the pack and slammed into Laura. She crashed to the ground.

A loud roaring sound suddenly filled her ears. Laura smelled gasoline and hot rubber. Still on the ground, she rolled onto her side just as a shiny black Suzuki Hayabusa rumbled down the narrow alley. Laura hugged the wall to avoid being run over.

Then she heard Emiko scream.

As the motorcycle streaked by, Laura saw the rider. He was wearing black leather and a helmet with a red curved lightning bolt emblazoned on its tinted visor.

The cyclist reached out his arm and snatched up Emiko. The grab knocked the wind out of her, so the girl couldn't even call for help. As she was whisked away, the yellow plastic Matsukuwa slipped from her outstretched hand and shattered on the concrete.

Laura watched the motorcycle speed away with its helpless captive, the skateboarders following in the monster machine's wake.

CHAPTER 8

OUTSIDE THE KUP KAKE CLUB, TOKYO, JAPAN

Laura was astounded when Tom rolled around the corner on a skateboard. She scrambled to her feet and rushed to him. He dismounted and heel-kicked the board and caught it in midair.

"They took Emiko," Laura cried, pointing in the direction of the gang's retreat. "We were trapped by a bunch of guys on skateboards. Then a guy on the back of a motorcycle came through here and snatched her."

Tom burned with anger. "Did you see his face?"

"Just a helmet," she replied—then remembered a detail. "The helmet had lightning bolts on it. And he was wearing a leather jacket."

Tom cursed. Laura didn't know why, but she suspected that he knew the identity of the kidnapper.

"Mitch will be here any second," Tom told her. "I want both of you to go back to Shibuya Station together. Take the first train back to the Empire Hotel. Wake Mr. Chance up if you have to, and tell him what happened."

"Where—"

Tom hopped back on his board, ignoring her question. "I'm going after her," he yelled over the noise. Then he hopped onto the board and was gone.

Tom wasn't even out of sight when Mitch rolled around the bend. He raced to follow his brother, but Laura flagged him down. Impatiently he screeched to a halt and dismounted.

Laura told Mitch what had happened and what Tom had commanded them to do.

"You go back," growled Mitch. "I'm going after my brother."

"That's not what Tom wants. . . ."

"Tom's fifteen minutes older, but that doesn't make him the boss!" Mitch declared. "You go home. Tell Mr. Chance that Tom and I went after Emiko."

Before she could stop him, Mitch sped away.

"Stupid boys," she said, dusting herself off.

Suddenly aware of the spookiness of her surroundings, Laura hurried back to the lights and the crowds on Koen-dori Street.

She decided not to wait until she got home to speak with Mr. Chance and called him on her cell phone instead.

She explained what happened and told him where he could find her. Then Laura hung up and slipped the phone into her bag, next to her own Matsukuwa. She almost pulled the plastic phone out to call Emiko, but remembered that her friend's own Matsukuwa had been smashed.

Laura looked up and saw Miss Nikki in the crowd. She pushed forward to catch up with her teacher, but Miss Nikki saw her coming and hurried off the other way. Laura soon lost sight of her.

It was definitely Miss Nikki. But why was she here? Did it have something to do with Emiko's abduction? Laura wondered. Then she shook her head. I'm being silly. Every other teenager in Japan is here, why not Miss Nikki?

With a tired sigh, Laura gave up the chase and hurried back to Shibuya Station.

It was nearly ten o'clock when she arrived, but the throngs were still thick around the statue of Hachiko. It took Laura a while, but she eventually found a spot under the shadow of the loyal dog where she could sit and wait for Mr. Chance.

While she waited, Laura tried to convince herself that what had happened was just an elaborate prank. She imagined that Emiko would appear any minute, probably on the back of the motorcycle, laughing and talking with the cute guy who'd punked her.

Laura was still hoping her friend would magically appear when Mr. Chance arrived to take her home.

侍

Tom raced through the narrow alley for many, many blocks. Occasionally he would catch a glimpse of a skateboarder or two in the distance, right before they disappeared around a bend in the road.

Struggling to catch up, Tom pushed his own board to its limit. The ride was bumpy along the uneven roadway.

Suddenly the alley ended, and he roared onto an empty parking lot. Ahead of him, nestled between two skyscrapers, Tom spied a high-rise parking garage adjacent to a busy highway. On its roof he saw figures in black robes calmly watching his approach.

Tom swerved into the garage and raced up a spiral ramp to the roof. He found the skateboard gang standing in a circle, waiting for him. Kunio was there too, wearing black leather motorcycle gear and clutching a helmet with a red lightning bolt on the visor. There was no sign of the Suzuki Hayabusa, nor of Emiko.

Tom rolled to a halt and dismounted, facing the gang.

"Hello, Gai-jin," Kunio cried. "I told you what would happen the next time we met." He extended his arm and gave Tom a thumbs-down.

"Your threats don't scare me," replied Tom. "I want the girl."

Kunio feigned surprise. "Girl? I see no girl here."

"Emiko. You snatched her. I want her back," Tom repeated, his tone uncompromising.

"How about a race, then?" Kunio suggested. "Down the ramp."

"Just give me Emiko and I'll go," said Tom.

"Not on the roadway, of course," Kunio added. "But along the rail."

Tom studied the spiral ramp he'd just climbed. The guardrail was six feet high and bordered the ramp from the roof to the ground, eight stories below. It was concrete, with a flat surface on top about three feet wide. The racecourse was so narrow he and Kunio would barely be able to pass each other. If one of them lost their balance, there was nothing to prevent him from plunging off the ramp to his doom.

To add to the danger, six steel poles topped by illuminated glass balls were intermittently spaced in the middle of the guardrail. A collision with one of them would end the competition—and in the blink of an eye, someone's life.

"A race for the girl, Gai-jin. Or are you afraid?" Kunio said scornfully.

Tom weighed his options and realized he didn't

have any. "Deal," he agreed.

Tom climbed the guardrail, board in hand. While he waited for his opponent, he examined the racecourse. Nervously, he glanced over the side, at the paved parking lot five hundred feet below.

"Who takes the inside lane?" Tom asked.

It was a wise question. The racer on the inside would have a distinct advantage. If he fell, it would only be six feet to the circular ramp. Falling the other way would be fatal.

Kunio waved disdainfully. "You take the inside lane, Gai-jin. You need all the help you can get."

Kunio's gang laughed at the insult. Then they circled their leader. As he donned his helmet, another boarder leaned close to Kunio's ear.

"Good news, Kunio-san," he whispered. "Two men wait at the bottom of the ramp to ambush Thomas. Even if he wins, the Gai-jin will lose."

Kunio sneered. "He will not win. But they are welcome to finish him off, if I don't do it first."

The crowd parted and Kunio climbed onto the concrete wall. Tom eyed his opponent. Kunio's expression was invisible under his tinted visor.

Another skateboarder with long, spiky hair ran into the center of the ramp.

"Get ready!" he commanded.

Tom set the board down on the concrete, using his heel to tilt it so the wheels didn't meet the pavement.

"Three . . . two . . . one . . . GO!"

Kunio jabbed his elbow into Tom's chest the second the race began. Tom had expected such a move and deflected the blow. But the attack cost him a critical second, and Kunio took the lead.

The concrete surface had hidden bumps that vibrated the skateboard under his sneakers and threatened to throw him off course, as he leaned precariously to keep the board on a circular path. Tom closed in on his opponent.

Kunio's shoulder brushed the first light pole, which slowed him down. Tom zoomed around the same post without touching it and so maintained his speed. By the time the racers reached the second pole, Tom was overtaking his rival.

Kunio swiveled his head, saw Tom closing. He

laughed behind his visor. Then he butted the electric light with his helmet.

The ball exploded in a shower of sparks and glass. Directly behind Kunio, sparks rained down on Tom, and he was pelted with razor-sharp shards. He closed his eyes to protect them—and nearly went over the side.

When he opened his eyes again, Tom saw flames licking his sweatshirt. He smelled scorching hair. Wobbling on his board, he beat out the fire and kept on going.

Kunio slowed, and Tom caught up to him near the third pole—only to realize that the gang leader was about to pull the same trick.

SMASH!

More sparks, more splintered glass came at him. This time Tom deftly dodged most of it and surged ahead. They were halfway down the ramp now, and Tom was on Kunio's tail.

Tom decided not to wait for another dirty trick. He tucked his arms close to his sides and crouched low, picking up speed. As they approached the fourth light post, he slammed his board into Kunio and pushed out with both arms.

Kunio slammed right into the steel pole. Tom saw the crash, heard Kunio's helmet crack. The move almost caused Tom to topple over the side, but he regained his balance and raced around the light.

He stole a glance over his shoulder and saw the skateboard shoot out from under Kunio's feet and plunge to the parking lot far below.

Kunio tumbled off the guardrail and hit the ramp. Tom saw the gang run to their leader's side as Kunio jumped to his feet and tore the broken helmet off his head. Then Tom raced around the next circle and they were out of sight.

"Yes!" Tom cried, throwing up his arm and clenching his fist in a victory salute. He was relieved to see Kunio unharmed, but happier to win. The wheels rumbled under his feet, the wind rippled his hair as Tom swerved around another light post.

All I have to do is reach the bottom of the ramp, and they'll turn Emiko loose, he mused. And boarding down the rest of the way should be pretty easy without Kunio trying to kill me.

CHAPTER 9

HIWA PARKING GARAGE, SHIBUYA DISTRICT

Mitch rolled out of the alley in time to see Kunio's board shatter on the pavement. He saw his brother, too. Tom was racing down the ramp on the guardrail, wheels striking sparks off the concrete.

Then Mitch spotted two men armed with nunchakus waiting at the bottom of the ramp to take Tom down. The punks were so intent on their prey they didn't notice Mitch's arrival.

Their funeral, Mitch thought.

He rolled inside the parking garage and slammed his board into the shin of one guy, who went down clutching his leg. His nunchakus clattered to the ground. Mitch kept rolling, bowling the other kid over with a head butt. The punk flipped over a trash can, spilling its contents.

Mitch jumped off his speeding board, and it careened against the guardrail. He faced his opponents, but they appeared to be down for the count.

Tom roared off the ramp a split second later. The sudden stop threw him off the board. He stumbled, arms windmilling, but did not fall.

"Dude, you're a mess," Mitch declared.

Tom's sweatshirt was scorched and a chunk of hair was burned away from his scalp. There were cuts on his head and burn marks on the side of his face. Mitch knew his brother was hurting, but to his surprise, Tom was grinning.

"I won, dude!" Tom cried. "I beat Kunio."

Mitch heard shouts of rage and glanced over his shoulder. The gang was charging down the ramp, Kunio in the lead. Some of them were waving fighting sticks and links of chain. Others shook clenched fists.

"I don't think they're coming to award you a prize. We better get out of here, pronto," Mitch warned.

"But Kunio said he'd turn Emiko over to me if I won," protested Tom.

"He lied. Get over it and run!" Mitch replied.

He grabbed his brother's arm and shoved him. Tom took off, limping slightly. Mitch knew Kunio's boys would overtake them in under a minute. They needed reinforcements, and Mitch knew just how to get them.

Hopping over the tumbled trash can, Mitch scrambled to a fire alarm on the wall and yanked the lever. Immediately the garage filled with the piercing howl of a hundred sirens. Emergency lights sprang to life, illuminating every level of the concrete structure with flashing red lights. In the distance, Mitch heard weird, warbling sirens and knew the police and fire department were on their way.

The alarms had the desired effect on Kunio and his punks. The gang scattered in a dozen different directions to escape before the authorities arrived. Mitch ran too, and caught up with Tom at the entrance to the alley.

"I think we lost them," Mitch cried.

"I won," growled Tom, clenching his fists.

Mitch rested a hand on his brother's shoulder. "Let's find a train and go home, bro."

侍

"Ouch!" Tom cried, wincing.

Laura plunked another glass splinter into the bathroom sink and dropped her tweezers.

"I think that's the last of the glass," she declared, dabbing the wound on Tom's forehead with soft cotton.

The pain was easing, but Tom was agitated about more than a few cuts. "Kunio said he'd give Emiko back and he lied. She's just a teenager. What could he want with her?"

"Mr. Chance has a theory," Laura replied.

While the brothers waited for her to elaborate, Laura

twisted the cap on a tube of burn cream.

"Come on, spill it!" Mitch urged.

"Give me a second," she said. She touched the cool salve to the skin on Tom's neck, then gently rubbed it in.

"Emiko Gensai is the daughter of Dr. Hideki Gensai, a geologist and explorer of South Pacific islands," Laura explained. "Dr. Gensai is also a renowned volcanologist."

Tom made a face. "So you're telling me Emiko's dad is an expert on Mr. Spock?"

"No!" cried Mitch. "Laura's telling you that the comic book that Kim Tanukis wrote must be true. Why else would Julian Vane need a volcanologist—that's an expert on volcanoes, dumbo—unless he's planning to set off Fuji?"

"That's what Mr. Chance thinks too," Laura said. "He left here an hour ago to see Dr. Gensai, who lives in Kobe. He wants to know if the doctor has been contacted by the kidnappers—"

"Wait a minute," Tom interrupted, fidgeting under Laura's fussing. "I haven't heard the name Julian Vane mentioned around here, except by us."

"No," Laura said. "He's in the *doujinshi*—"

"Not even there!" Tom shot back. "The villain in the comic book had some crazy name that only sounded similar."

Mitch shook his head.

"Look, we *deduced* it was Julian Vane," Tom protested. "But the real villain here is Kunio and his gang. They're the ones who took Emiko."

Mitch said nothing. He couldn't argue with Tom's logic. Laura shrugged and put more cream on Tom's burns.

"I knew Kunio was trouble the moment I saw the lightning bolt tattoo over his eye," said Tom. "What kind of nut has a tattoo on his head?"

Laura blinked in surprise. "Apparently, a nut like you," she told him.

"Huh?"

Laura pulled her hand away. "Some of your hair burned away. There's a tattoo on the back of your neck."

Tom snatched a hand mirror off the sink and used it to examine the mark.

"She's right, dude. I see it too," said Mitch.

Dumbfounded, Tom could only nod. The tattoo was there, for sure. A nickel-size design in the shape of a cat's claw.

"What the . . . ?" Tom was so shocked that he couldn't even finish his sentence.

"Wait a minute, that looks like a cat's claw! Ring any bells? Cat's Claw Clan—that's Dad's R.O.N.I.N. clan!" Mitch announced with excitement.

"So you think it's a marking that Cat's Claw members have?" Tom asked.

"There's only one way to find out," Mitch answered. "Laura, check out the back of my neck."

Laura walked over and pulled Mitch's shaggy hair to either side so the bottom of his neck was visible. "Yup, you have one too. A cat's claw."

"This is either really cool or really spooky," Mitch remarked.

"What are you talking about? This is awesome!" Tom cried, excitedly. "I've always wanted a tattoo, but Dad always said 'over my dead body.' I can't believe he knew I already had one the whole time."

"Hey, wait a minute. If we have tattoos of our clans, you must have one of yours too, Laura. Come here, let me check your neck." Mitch lifted up Laura's blue-black hair and pushed it over her shoulder.

He was nervous about being so close to Laura, but he quickly checked for her tattoo. "There's nothing there," he said. "But that doesn't make any sense. You must have one."

He looked once more, wondering if he had missed it. Suddenly he spotted something small and white hiding behind her left earlobe, just above her jaw line. "Wait, I see something! It looks like a crane, a white crane."

"My father loves white cranes," she said. "They're his favorite animal."

"Well, now we know why," announced Tom. "Looks like you and your dad probably belong to the White Crane Clan, or something like that, anyway."

"Are you sure you don't think this is creepy yet?" Mitch asked, hoping someone else felt the same way he did.

"Let's just focus on getting our dads back," Laura said. "Then hopefully all of this will start making some sense."

侍

Mitch waited for Brian Saito outside room 101 before class the next morning. His friend arrived at the last minute, bleary-eyed and disheveled.

"Man, what a night I had," Brian crowed.

"Were you in Shibuya?" Mitch demanded. "Did you call Emiko on a Matsukuwa?"

Brian shook his head. "Never left the house. And those things are for girls. I don't own one."

Mitch told him about the call but left out the part about the kidnapping and the chase that followed.

"Did you mention Laura and Emiko to any of your friends?" Mitch asked.

"I don't have any friends," replied Brian. "And that's what I've been trying to tell you. I was sitting at my computer last night, doing homework, when some girl instant-messaged me—"

"So?"

"She's from the advanced program," Brian explained. "She said she heard a lot about me and wanted to get together once I moved into the dorm."

"That's crazy," Mitch said. "This girl doesn't even know you, and you don't know her."

"Her name's Yuki and she told me all about the labs, the workshops. We messaged each other practically all night." Brian grinned. "Man, I can't wait—"

The bell rang, signaling the start of class. They rushed to take their seats. Because of the rules of silence, they couldn't speak again until after class. But it really didn't matter anymore, because Mitch believed Brian's story. More than that, he thought Brian's new girlfriend "Yuki" was like that call from the Kup Kake Club—an elaborate lie meant to entrap him.

"Now that we are all here, the lesson can begin," the disembodied voice announced. "Today you will be tested on software application skills."

The monitor on Mitch's handmade computer sprang to life.

"On the screen you will see a long instructional

program used to guide an automated system," the voice said. "Under it you'll find a second code created by one of our advanced students."

Mitch gazed at the screen. The long code began with the words *Tōkyō Denryoku Kabushiki-gaisha*, which he didn't understand. But he recognized the words in front of the second code: Kim Tanukis, Code Seven.

So that's where Kim went, Mitch thought. No wonder we couldn't find her. She vanished into the program. Brian said the students in the advanced classes were too cool for school.

"Your assignment is to plant the second code inside the first, altering the original automated program without detection," the voice commanded. "You have three hours. Begin now."

Brian went right to work. But for a long time Mitch just stared at his screen. His assignment was to launch a Trojan Horse, a type of program that caused other computers to malfunction.

What the voice is ordering me to do is wrong, and maybe illegal, Mitch mused. Why would a legitimate corporation like Matsu Cybernetics want to mess with a dangerous program?

Mitch decided that the only way to answer his own question was to follow the assignment and see what happened next. He figured it would be safe. Whatever virus or malware he unleashed would be trapped inside his junkyard computer, where it could do no harm.

侍

In room 324, Laura's art class began without Emiko Gensai. Miss Nikki assigned them a new project and the other students went to work.

But Laura couldn't concentrate. She watched Miss Nikki, wondering just what her teacher had been doing in Shibuya last night, around the bend from the spot where Emiko was snatched.

It seemed like an incredible coincidence for Miss Nikki to be present at that exact time and place—too incredible, in fact. The more Laura thought about it, the more she became convinced that Miss Nikki knew something about her friend's disappearance.

Twice Miss Nikki caught Laura watching her. Laura expected to be corrected by her stern teacher for rude behavior. But both times Nikki Matsu looked away, pretending not to notice—and that made Laura more suspicious than ever.

CHAPTER 10

MATSU CYBERNETICS BUILDING, TOKYO, JAPAN

Nikki Matsu tried to enter the secret elevator in the teachers' lounge but found the door that led to it blocked by a pair of floating Eyes. The sentinels spun in the air to face her and directed their lenslike optical sensors at her face. A light flashed and Nikki blinked.

"Can we help you, Miss Matsu?" the Eyes asked in unison. Nikki realized they'd taken a retinal scan to identify her.

"I need to go to my father's office," Nikki replied.

"CEO Matsu is not present—"

"I need to get something I left in his office," she said impatiently.

"Not possible," the machines answered in evenly modulated electronic voices. "Vital upgrades are currently underway inside the CEO's office. The elevator has been deactivated."

Nikki had no choice but to leave. Still haunted by her suspicions, she returned to her tiny faculty office on the top floor of the school. She used her keycard to unlock the electric door, but when it slid aside she was startled to find Laura waiting for her, with twin brothers she didn't recognize.

"Miss Nikki, we have to talk," Laura said.

Nikki nodded. She'd known this moment would come when Laura spotted her on the street the night before. To her surprise, Nikki felt relieved to share some of the secrets she'd been keeping with someone—even perfect strangers.

侍

As soon as the door closed, Tom fired off his first question to Nikki Matsu.

"Is Kunio your brother?" he asked.

Nikki blinked, puzzled.

"I saw the trophy case in the solarium this morning," Tom explained. "Kunio's picture is under the prize he won at last year's national skateboard competition. His last name is the same as yours."

Nikki nodded. "Kunio is my cousin." She pushed her bangs aside and showed them her own lightning bolt tattoo over her eye.

"I've got one too," said Tom. "But this is no time for show-and-tell." It occurred to him that Nikki's lightning bolt tattoo could be connected to R.O.N.I.N., just like theirs was. But then he was reminded of Kunio's tattoo, and he decided he'd better not say anything, just in case.

"My father became a businessman," Nikki told them. "Kunio's father turned to a life of crime, became a yakuza—"

"A who-za?" Tom asked.

"It's like the mafia, only Japanese," explained Mitch.

"That is so," said Nikki. "When his father was murdered in a gang war, my father accepted Kunio into the school."

Mitch snorted. "Talk about family ties. Where is Kunio now?"

"He and his gang have taken the corporate helicopter to the research station at Mount Fuji. To witness a science demonstration, supposedly."

"Does your father know Kunio is a kidnapper?" Tom asked.

Nikki lowered her eyes. "I hope he does not, but—"

"But what?" Laura cried.

"For weeks I have attended weekly video conferences with my father," Nikki told the others. "But recently I realized that all that time I have been speaking to an avatar—a digital ghost that looks and sounds like my father. But this ghost is really a demon who commands us to do evil things."

Tom's eyes narrowed. "Like kidnap Emiko Gensai?"

Nikki nodded. "I believe now that my father himself is a captive, and that his associate—a man named Julian Vane—has been using the digital avatar to trick me *and* Kunio. The image Vane uses is not perfect, however. I recognized the flaws."

"You would," said Laura.

"Do you know Kim Tanukis?" Mitch asked.

Nikki nodded again. "She is a student in the advanced cybernetics program."

"But Kim didn't really draw that *doujinshi*, did she?" asked Laura.

"No. I did," Nikki confessed. "I wrote it as a warning to the outside world. We are watched all the time at the Matsu School. It was the only way I could get the message to the world."

"Emiko's father is an expert on volcanoes," Tom said. "Was she kidnapped so her father would create an eruption at Mount Fuji?"

Nikki frowned. "I fear Julian Vane plans something much worse than setting off a volcano. I am sure Emiko was taken because of her skills as a digital artist."

Nikki faced Laura. "You saw Emiko's art. It was truly astonishing. Julian Vane must have seen her work too. The digital image of my father *almost* fooled me. And if Emiko had worked on it, I would have been convinced the avatar really was my father."

"I saw a program you created today," said Mitch. "It was designed to override another program code used by—here, I wrote it down."

Mitch handed Nikki a scrap of paper. She read it and gasped. "*Tōkyō Denryoku Kabushiki-gaisha*. That's the Tokyo Electric Power Company!"

"So Vane plans to disrupt Tokyo's power grid," Tom guessed.

"No," cried Nikki. "The last time I was in my father's office, I noticed that a new computer had been installed. A type of automated control mainframe used in every nuclear reactor in Japan—"

"Whoa!" Mitch exclaimed. "If the Shinshi code was broadcast from that computer—"

"Julian Vane would control every nuclear reactor in the nation," Nikki finished. "He could override the safety controls and push the reactors into a meltdown. Millions could be harmed!"

"Not if we can help it," stated Tom. "We'll go up to your father's office right now and shut that computer down!"

"Better yet," Mitch said, "I created a shredder program that will blow that mainframe's mind and delete the Shinshi code in the process."

"It's impossible," said Nikki. "There's no way up to the office. The elevator is deactivated. Sentinel

Eyes guard the door. And more of the Eyes are guarding the executive suite."

"We should wait for Mr. Chance to come back," Laura suggested. "He'll know what to do."

"No time," declared Mitch. "Vane has sealed off the tower, which means he's about to launch the program."

"But the only way to reach my father's office would be to climb the glass spire itself," said Nikki. "And that would be crazy."

"Crazy is my business," Tom told her.

侍

Mitch and Tom clung to a catwalk near the top of the Matsu Cybernetics Building, high above the city. Howling winds threatened to tear them from their precarious perch. The afternoon sun was bright, but at such a high altitude a bone-chilling cold traveled on the wind.

Mitch stared up at the glass spire looming over them. Then he examined the fragile-looking ladder that ran up the side, all the way to CEO Inoshiro Matsu's executive suite, according to Nikki.

"Maybe we should both make the climb!" Mitch shouted. He had to yell to be heard over the wind.

"No way, Motormouth," replied Tom. "I'm going to have a tough enough time getting up there myself. I don't need to drag you along with me."

"But—"

"Think, dude," Tom insisted. "Don't you remember what happened the last time we went rock climbing?"

Mitch looked sheepish. "Yeah. I fell off."

"So it's better if I go it alone," said Tom.

Mitch nodded reluctantly. "You have your pocket pal? The memory stick with the shredder code, right?" he asked.

Tom patted his jacket. "Here in my pocket."

"And the Matsukuwa? We'll need it to communicate."

Tom displayed his toy phone. "Couldn't you have found another color besides pink? It's so . . . girly."

"Best I could do on short notice, dude," Mitch replied. He examined his brother's safety line, then looked over the side at the street far below. "If you fall, I'll catch you and I won't let go."

"Don't worry," Tom said. "I'm not going to let anything happen to me before I ask Mr. Chance how we got these nutty tattoos on our necks."

They chuckled, then shook hands.

"Good luck. And watch out for those Eyes in the Sky," Mitch warned. "They can't go outside the building or they lose power. But once you're on the inside, they can get you."

"I'll only be in the office for a minute," said Tom. "I won't make a sound, and I'll be gone before the Eyes know I was even there."

CHAPTER 11

THE SPIRE, MATSU CYBERNETICS BUILDING

Tom's arms felt like lead and his legs like jelly when he finally reached the ventilation grill above the CEO's executive office. His face was windburned, hands raw from gripping the cold steel rungs.

He looped one arm around the ladder and fumbled for the pink phone with the other.

"I'm here," he yelled into the Matsukuwa.

He could barely hear Mitch's voice over the moaning wind.

"Unscrew the lock on the ventilation grill," Mitch replied. "According to the blueprints, it should open up like a door. The shaft should be large enough for you to enter."

"Like a tunnel rat," muttered Tom.

"What?" Mitch asked.

"Nothing. I'm signing off," Tom answered. "I need both hands to use the pocket pal."

Tom tucked the phone into his pocket. Then he fished out the pocket pal, deployed the screwdriver tool, and set to work. In a few moments the grill was open, and Tom crawled into the shaft.

Away from the howling winds at last, Tom was oppressed by a dark silence. Dragging his safety line behind him, Tom moved deeper inside the aluminum vent.

So far the blueprints Nikki provided were accurate. The vent was wide enough for Tom to crawl through—barely—but it seemed pretty flimsy, too. Tom wondered if the metal would be able to support his weight.

He was cautiously inching forward when the floor beneath him suddenly gave way. In a shower of plaster, soundproof panels, and shattered fluorescent light fixtures, he dropped through the ceiling and landed on top of a huge polished oak desk the size of Mr. Chance's PT Cruiser.

Tom heard alarm bells ringing from the other side of the wall. So much for stealth, he mused.

Then he realized he was inside the CEO's office. He spied the computer control station, recognizing it from the picture Nikki had shown him in the Matsu industrial catalog. The machine was alive and ticking, but still in countdown mode. Tom rolled off the desk and ran to its side.

It took him a moment, but he found a USB port and shoved the memory stick into the slot.

At first nothing happened. Then the computer

screen, which had been scrolling streams of data, went haywire—and then blank. A moment later the digital clock froze, and Tom knew the computer and the deadly program it contained were fried.

"Mission accomplished," Tom said into the Matsukuwa.

"I can hear the alarm bells down here," Mitch replied. "Get out of there now."

Tom used the safety rope to haul himself back up, into the vent. He quickly crawled toward the sunlight, pausing to rest before beginning the long descent.

Suddenly, over the whistling wind, Tom heard a crash and saw a swarm of Eyes racing toward him through the vent. He swung his legs over the side, but before he could grab the ladder, the first shiny metal globe slammed into him.

The impact knocked the wind out of him. Desperately he tried to hang on. But as the first Eye, now powerless, tumbled to the street below, another one soared out of the ventilation duct and struck his head.

Tom's fingers slipped and he felt himself falling. Then his world faded to black.

侍

"I'm here again," Tom realized. "I'm back on the island."

He could smell the sea air and feel the high winds

whipping around the lone mountaintop. The symbol of R.O.N.I.N. loomed over him, a majestic jade dragon with glowing emeralds for eyes, the mysterious cave entrance hidden behind it.

Then Tom heard the sound of insistent beating; it was coming from helicopter blades. Like hungry raptors, the black choppers swarmed the island. Circling the mountain, they swooped closer and closer with each new pass.

Finally one of the choppers bucked, and a missile arrowed toward him, a white plume painting its path through the night. Tom gasped as the rocket slammed the side of the mountain. The fiery explosion shook rocks loose, sent them tumbling down the sheer cliffs.

A moment later he was deep inside the cave again, within the vast jade chamber.

"Oh, no! The Scroll!" called a voice from the cave entrance. The dragon's voice!

Then the voice of the dragon spoke again.

"Thomas . . . you must save them! You and your brother! Do you understand?"

Men in black battle suits surged past the jade dragon and into the cave, machine guns raised.

"No! Save what?"

侍

Tom's own cry shook him back to consciousness and brought Mitch and Mr. Chance racing to his side.

"Dude, what's wrong?" Mitch cried.

"It's the scroll! I think someone's trying to take it!"

"Another dream," declared Mr. Chance.

Tom blinked, surprised to find himself in his bed at the hotel. Outside, the sky was dark and the lights of Tokyo gleamed in the moonlight.

"What happened? Did I dream the whole thing?" Tom murmured.

"I told you I'd never let go of that safety line," Mitch said, displaying the bandages on his hands. "FYI, rope burns really hurt."

"Not as much as my head," Tom groaned. "Please tell me it was worth it."

"Your sacrifices, such as they were, were not in *vain*, if you will pardon my pun," Mr. Chance said.

Tom and Mitch rolled their eyes at each other.

"I am proud to say that you fried the computer before the codes were broadcast," Mr. Chance continued. "You saved countless lives."

Tom sighed. "But I'll bet you still don't know where that creep Kunio is, and you haven't found Emiko yet."

Mr. Chance frowned. "Not Emiko, nor her father Dr. Gensai, who has been taken too." Then the man grinned. "But we should be grateful. You have both entered the tiger's den and saved one of its cubs."

Tom blinked. "You mean Nikki Matsu?"

Mr. Chance nodded. "Nikki has joined our fight. It seems as though she is convinced that Vane is also behind the disappearance of her father, that he is being held hostage."

"He wouldn't be the first one," Tom added.

"Very true, young sir. Vane seems to be somehow connected to all of these mysterious disappearances. We must continue to follow him until he leads us to what we are seeking. We must first uncover his next big move."

"And then we follow him there," Tom agreed without hesitation.

"There is one more thing," Mr. Chance said.

"What?" Mitch asked.

"I have discovered a clue that may help us make sense of your dreams, Tom," Mr. Chance informed the brothers. "A map I found in the office of the missing Dr. Gensai, along with some logs of his journeys and some ocean charts."

Mitch tried scratching his head with thickly bandaged hands. "A map?"

"To a South Sea island shrouded in fog," explained Mr. Chance. "Where a dragon sits on a cliff at the top of a mountain—"

Tom jumped out of bed and grabbed Mr. Chance by the arms. "The island in my dream!" he cried. "Where is it? We have to go there!"

"The map is incomplete," Mr. Chance cautioned. "It will be difficult to find the island without help from the man who drew it."

"Then we have to find Dr. Gensai now!" Tom urged. "If we find him, we can find the island."

"If I am not mistaken, our trail of Julian Vane should lead us to Dr. Gensai," replied Mr. Chance. "Then we shall begin our journey to the island shrouded in fog, or Dragon Island, as it is called, the place where the sacred Dragon Scroll is kept. But for now, get some rest, and heal. Tomorrow we will begin our search."

DON'T MISS THE NEXT
47 R.O.N.I.N ADVENTURE:

EPISODE 3 - THE GETAWAY

Like a well-fed cat, Julian Vane yawned and stretched his tanned, muscular body. He was reclining on a lounge chair under partly cloudy skies, but he wasn't on a beach. Vane's personal sun deck was located hundreds of feet in the air, around the outside perimeter of a saucer-shaped superstructure.

The saucer itself housed five large floors of computer labs and the most cutting-edged communications technology available on Earth. Spearing these oval-shaped floors was a supporting tower of stone and steel. At its core was a sleek, superfast elevator; and rising above it all was a massive broadcast antennae that reached so high into the sky it disappeared into the clouds.

Vane was very proud of his brand-new communications building, his "Space Needle of the open Pacific," as he sometimes referred to it.

But this Space Needle is going to achieve something no one on Earth has ever seen before, he thought with deep satisfaction. Only now, with the use of digital technology, can a man like me make the world believe whatever I decide it should. . . .

"Your drink, Mr. Vane," a feminine voice sang out in a heavy Russian accent.

Vane slipped on his mirrored sunglasses and slowly sat up. Without a word, he took the tall frosted glass from the beautiful woman wearing a bikini and sandals.

"Not sweet enough," Vane said after trying a sip. "Take it away. And don't bring it back until it's *right*."

"Yes, Mr. Vane, sir."

Vane selected a bottle of suntan lotion and snapped his fingers. A Spanish woman in a bikini rushed up to him.

"Scalp," was all he said.

"*Si*, Mr. Vane," said the woman.

The woman took the bottle and set to work, massaging the sunblock onto Vane's shaved head.

"That's enough," he said, waving her away as if she'd suddenly become as annoying as a fly.

Leaning back in his lounge chair, he reached for his remote control and flipped channels on his custom-made broadcast receiver.

Vane's personal flat screen televisions were so advanced they could pick up signals from any broadcast, anywhere in the world. This particular model included special coatings and pixelation enhancements, so Vane could see a clear, vibrant picture, even in direct sunlight.

" . . . and that's the reaction from London on the World Freedom Concert," a British announcer declared. "Now let's go to Theresa Parker, our BBC correspondent in the Middle East . . . "

Click! Vane switched to a news channel in China. His Mandarin was rusty so he pushed another button and the words were instantly translated into English.

" . . . and officials say the new transit system will be in place within five years, thus addressing the growing concerns of traffic congestion. In other news, a concert promoting World Freedom will be held . . . "

Click, click, click . . .

" . . . and the excitement is building about the World Freedom Concert. Just announced this morning, the concert's been in the planning stages for many months. Funded by an anonymous philanthropist, the event is being billed as a giant Olympics of music, with hundreds of performers in dozens of nations . . . "

"Good, very good . . . ," mumbled Vane. He settled back and smiled. It's all coming together, he thought. After years of planning, everything is falling into place. . . .

"Mr. Vane-*san,* sir?"

Vane didn't bother turning his freshly lotioned head to see who had spoken to him. He immediately recognized the young voice of the Japanese teenager Kunio Matsu.

"Yes, Kunio. Come closer. My assistant buzzed me that you were on your way up."

Kunio stepped farther out onto the sun deck and

bowed deeply. He appeared to be holding steady, but sweat had formed on the peach fuzz of the teen's upper lip. Vane could see he was nervous about something.

Just then, Vane's bikini-clad Russian waitress brought his drink back. "Here you are, sir," she purred. "It's much sweeter now."

Vane took the drink, sipped, then waved the woman away dismissively. Kunio's head remained forward, but his eyes followed the woman's retreating form.

"All right, Kunio," said Vane. "You know I don't like my time wasted. So *get* to the point."

"I've just come from Tokyo. It seems your Black Lotus ninjas were ambushed by a gang of White Lotus ninjas, sir, while they were tracking the escaped prisoner . . . " Kunio's voice trailed off. He swallowed with obvious nervousness.

"So Rosso knows of my plans," Vane announced, not so much for Kunio's benefit, but for his own. "The news got to him a bit sooner than I had hoped; the other matter isn't quite ready yet. It was Chance, I'm sure of it. He always was a huge thorn in my side. Is that all, Kunio?" he demanded.

"No, sir. During the fight, the Black Ninjas lost the prisoner's trail. He managed to escape again, and no one can find him anywhere. They've searched the city."

Kunio's voice trailed off. He swallowed with obvious nervousness.

Vane threw his sweet island drink across the sun deck. The tall, frosted glass smashed against the balcony rail. Sharp shards flew in all directions. Kunio winced but did not move a muscle as a few of the smaller glass pieces embedded themselves in one arm.

"Again!" Vane screamed. "This is a disgrace! I gave them one task. I need that man, otherwise the whole plan is at a standstill. You go back to them and you tell my captain to find him . . . or else."

"Or else, sir?"

Vane's voice went low. "Or else, they will start *paying* for each and every one of their mistakes."

Kunio responded with a flurry of bows. *"Hai,* Vane-*san.* I mean, *yes, sir,* Mr. Vane! I shall tell him. I shall make it very clear."

"While you're here, I want you to do something more for me."

"Yes, sir?"

"Dr. Gensai has cooperated fully. His research enabled us to tap into the energy trapped under this volcanic island. Now my broadcast tower and everything else on this island runs on geothermal energy, which means we are finally self-sustaining. We have limitless power, but . . . "

Vane sighed and shifted in his chair. "Dr. Gensai's daughter has not been so helpful, however. Talk to that silly girl with the pink hair."

"Emiko?"

Vane waved his hand. "Whatever."

"What would you like me to say?"

"She's being a brat. She won't do the work I require until she speaks with her father. She's gifted enough at computer graphics to recognize an avatar, so don't even try to fool her with a fake program. Just get a remote hookup to Dr. Gensai and make sure she's satisfied that he's alive and well treated. Once she knows that, tell her she had better do *everything* we say from now on, or the next time she sees her dear old dad in living color, she'll be forced to watch him being *tortured*. All right?"

Kunio nodded. "I'll arrange everything, Mr. Vane, sir."

"I know you will." Vane stood and approached the teenager. His voice became softer. "You know, Kunio, you're beginning to look a lot like your father. He was a handsome man, and a loyal, reliable solider. Before he died, he was well respected among the ranks of the Yakuza—and you could be too. I see great potential in you, Kunio, just like your father."

"Thank you, sir!"

"Now go and do as I ask. As always, I'll make sure you are *well* rewarded for your loyal service."

"Yes, Mr. Vane. Do not worry, sir. I am honored to do anything you ask. . . . "

Kunio Matsu left the Needle's sun deck and strode across the thick, Persian rugs of Julian Vane's private apartment.

One day, he thought, this could all be mine.

He admired the plush furnishings, the priceless sculptures and artwork, the curvaceous, long-legged servants. He took them all in with greedy eyes, and then he smiled at the uniformed man, standing guard by the elevator.

The guard scowled back.

Vane thinks I want to be like my father, Kunio thought as he stepped into the richly-paneled elevator, but my father was a fool. He wasn't smart enough to keep himself alive. Well, I'm smarter than that. And I want more than my father ever had. I want to live like this . . . like Vane, the billionaire king. And I'm ready to do just about anything to make that happen. . . .

侍

Three floors below Julian Vane's sun deck, Emiko Gensai was sitting in a chair, staring at the ocean, below the high window of her locked room.

When she heard the door suddenly bang open, she turned so fast her long, pink-streaked, black hair flew in all directions.

"Why did you have to start acting like a brat?"

demanded the young man standing at the door.

"Kunio Matsu!" Emiko cried, jumping to her feet. She pointed an accusing finger. "When I saw those masked thugs on skateboards coming at me and Laura, I should have *known* one of them was you. You're such a jerk!"

"Shut up!" Kunio shouted, entering the room and slamming the door behind him. "Kidnapping you was enough trouble—what with those stupid American brothers getting in my way! Now you've gone and irritated Mr. Vane, which is making *my* life even more difficult!"

"*Your* life! You've got nerve! Do you think I care one fig about your life? *You're* the brat, Kunio, not me!"

Emiko fell to the ground and curled up in a ball. She couldn't believe any of this was happening to her.

Within hours of being snatched off the Tokyo streets, she'd been transported to some sort of concrete bunker near Mount Fuji.

For hours, men in black jumpsuits kept her in a dank, dimly lit sub basement and then she found out that they had also kidnapped her father!

Once her father arrived at the Mount Fuji facility, the men forced the two of them to board a large helicopter at gunpoint. Then they were flown to this remote Pacific island.

Emiko's father had told her not to cry, to stay strong, and to cooperate. "We will get through this together, little one," he said. "Be brave."

She was scared, but she tried to do as her father asked.

It wasn't bad at first. After they arrived at the island, they were treated almost like guests in a grand hotel—except their adjoining rooms had locks on the outsides and two men standing guard around-the-clock.

Emiko was given a beautiful room with an incredible view of the ocean, a flat screen TV and DVD player. She had a closet of comfortable clothing and was served delicious meals. She was even allowed to swim in the ocean and walk on the beach, with a guard trailing her every move.

It actually wasn't too bad, and she was cooperating with their demands—until they took her dad away.

From the window, she watched them escort her father onto the beach and into a waiting ship. The ship sailed away and never returned. And that was when she rebelled.

She refused to do any more computer graphics work until she knew her father was okay. The guards scared her and threatened her, but she didn't care. They couldn't *force* her to do the work. They'd have to meet her demands or kill her, and if her father was already dead, then she was ready to die too.

"Why did you have to pick me? Why?"

"Because my cousin, Nikki, said you were the most gifted digital artist she'd ever known. That's why. The truth is . . . we could have put you into the Matsu School's advanced program and had you do our work there—"

"What! Do you mean to tell me that the advanced students are being duped into doing evil?"

"Of course! And we would have duped you, too, but your father is too valuable. We knew he'd never cooperate unless we threatened him with harming you, so you were kidnapped along with him. And we were right. Your dad's already cooperated fully. And now you're going to cooperate too. You're going to help Vane perfect his avatars."

Kunio walked over to the computer station in Emiko's room. Three flat screens were set up, each one was connected to a massive hard drive. All three drives were networked together and loaded with cutting-edged computer graphics software. It was a sweet setup for any computer science student.

Kunio tapped the keys and the monitors sprang to life. Three major world leaders flashed across the screen. The president of the United States appeared to be speaking from the Oval Office. The prime minister of England looked as though he were speaking from Ten Downing Street. And the Russian president appeared to be speaking from the Kremlin.

"I have to hand it to you, Emiko, these avatars are coming along nicely. . . . " Kunio toggled through more world leaders—the heads of China, Iran, India, Pakistan, Israel, and North and South Korea. "Vane had some pretty good graphics work going, but these are nearly flawless. You really are as good as Nikki claimed."

"Well, I don't care what your opinion is, Kunio. I don't care what you do to me, either. I'm not doing one more minute's work on those avatars until I know my father is all right."

"Yeah, yeah, I know. Listen, your father's fine, okay? Don't be a pain anymore. Look . . . "

Kunio pulled out his cell phone and pressed a speed dial.

"It's me, Kunio," he said to the person on the other end of the line. "Is Gensai ready to talk? Good. Put him on."

Kunio pressed the speaker function and held up the picture phone. "See? There he is. Talk to him: You'll see he's not an avatar. Your dad's okay."

"Father!" Emiko cried, running up to the phone. She reached out for the phone, but Kunio wouldn't let her hold it.

"Oh, no. I can't have you taking the phone and trying to call for help. Just talk to him over the speaker. He can see you too."

"Father, are you all right?" Emiko asked.

"Yes, yes, I'm fine. Please don't put yourself in danger. Cooperate, as I told you."

"Father, I have to know that it's really you. Can you tell me where we went on vacation last summer?"

Dr. Gensai nodded. A little smile lifted his lips. "We went to Disney World. The park in America's Florida."

"Do you remember what I bought before we left?"

"Mouse ears and a Cinderella headband."

Emiko began to cry. "Are you really okay, Father?"

"Yes, please don't cry. I can see how upset you are. They tell me we can talk every day . . . as long as you keep working on their computer graphics. Can you do that for me?"

"Yes, Father. I can . . . "

"Very good. That is very good." Dr. Gensai glanced away for a moment, then nodded. "I must say good-bye now, Emiko. Be brave."

"I will, Father. I love you."

"I love you, too, Emiko."

The call ended and Kunio smirked. "So you got what you wanted. Okay? Satisfied?"

"Hardly." Sniffling, Emiko turned away, wiping the tears off her face.

"Well, princess, let me make one thing very clear. If you don't start working on these avatars, you'll be seeing your father every day all right, only there will be less and less of him to see."

Emiko turned back and glared. "What do you mean by that?"

"I mean, if Julian Vane isn't happy about your progress, he's going to order his guards to start taking his anger out on your father."

"Noooooo!" Emiko cried. She launched herself at Kunio, but he just laughed at her ineffective punches. With ease, he threw her slight body to the floor before leaving the room.

Emiko sobbed as the guard slid the door lock back into place.

DYLAN SPROUSE AND COLE SPROUSE ARE TWO OF HOLLYWOOD'S MOST EMINENT RISING STARS.

Dylan and Cole were born in Arezzo, Italy, and currently reside in Los Angeles, California. Named for the jazz singer and pianist Nat King Cole, Cole's list of favorites includes math, the color blue, and animals. He also enjoys video games and all types of sports, including motocross, snowboarding, and surfing. Dylan, named after the poet Dylan Thomas, is very close to his brother and also has a great love of animals and video games. He enjoys science, the Los Angeles Lakers, and the color orange. He's a sports enthusiast and especially loves motocross, snowboarding, surfing, and basketball.

Cole and Dylan made their acting debuts on the big screen in *Big Daddy*, opposite Adam Sandler. Both also starred in *The Astronaut's Wife*, *Master of Disguise*, and *Eight Crazy Nights*. On television Cole and Dylan established themselves in the critically acclaimed ABC comedy series *Grace Under Fire* and eventually went on to star in NBC's *Friends* as David Schwimmer's son, Ben Geller.

Dylan and Cole currently star as the introspective Cody Martin and the mischievous Zack Martin, respectively, in the Disney Channel's amazingly successful sitcom *The Suite Life of Zack and Cody*, playing separate roles for the first time. Ranked number one in its time slot against all basic cable shows, *The Suite Life* is now one of the Disney Channel's top shows and is rapidly gaining worldwide success.

In September 2005 the Sprouses partnered with Dualstar Entertainment Group to launch the *Sprouse Bros.* brand, the only young men's lifestyle brand designed by boys for boys. The brand includes *Sprouse Bros. 47 R.O.N.I.N.*, an apparel collection, an online fan club, mobile content, a DVD series in development, and lots more in the works!